Wild Tides
Summer Adrift

E V McMillan

Color Your World Press, 2024

Some say. "Those who can't do, teach."
I say, for those things I can neither do nor teach,
I create characters who can.
~E V McMillan

To my family and friends, and all of the extraordinary
people who have supported me in this venture.

Also By E V McMillan

The Summer Adrift Series:

Shifting Tides

Wild Tides

Inherit the Tides

PROLOGUE·

San Diego, California, USA

The ocean was an endless sheet of glass, reflecting the late morning sun like a mirror.

Sitting on my surfboard, leaning forward, gripping the rails, and dangling my feet in the water, I took in the horizon and the sheer beauty of the Southern California coastline. Today was the last day of our vacation. Josh was flying to Johannesburg out of LAX to meet with execs at Walter Industries, one of our major sponsors, for some promo work tomorrow evening. Colin was going back home to Australia to check on family, and I had a few days before surfing the Pipeline in Hawaii. We'd free-surfed some of the most iconic spots along the Southern California coast from Ventura to San Diego, hitting seven beaches in ten days of pure relaxation, staying pretty much off the grid.

As I enjoyed the view and warm ocean water, I noticed Josh pointing at a drone that flew overhead. He seemed upset and gave Colin and me a thumbs-up, signaling he was heading back to shore. Always eager for a little friendly competition, Colin paddled toward him. Maybe I blinked or looked away for a second, I don't know, but seconds later, the ocean shattered into chaos. With an explosion of water, Josh was tossed high into the air, and his surfboard, still attached to the leash around his ankle, was broken into two pieces. My mouth dropped open, and my breath caught in my throat as I saw a dark gray horror rising from the depths—a great white shark, mouth gaping open like a baseball catcher's mitt, ready to catch Josh as he came back down.

Josh hit the water surface hard, his board smashing into his face, and the shark lunged repeatedly, hitting him and knocking him around like a ragdoll. It was a scene torn from nightmares.

Gut-wrenching panic clawed at me; my mind was racing, but my body was a statue of frozen terror. "Josh! Josh!" I screamed over and over, finally snapping out of my paralysis. I paddled furiously toward him as he flailed in the crimson-streaked water. Some other surfers had closed in behind me, their board slaps and shouts an ineffectual deterrent to the predator circling Josh.

With each stroke, my heart pounded a frantic drumbeat, and my focus narrowed solely on my friend, who had begun to pound on the shark's snout in a desperate bid for life. Then, suddenly, he was yanked downward into the ocean's dark abyss, and I screamed his name over and over.

When we reached him— me, several other surfers, and a few paddle-boarders—we converged in a protective ring around the blood-soaked patch of ocean where Josh had disappeared. As if he had been spit out, he resurfaced, clinging to the tattered remnants of his board, and I grabbed him and held on to him. Adrenaline gave way to a brief, shaky relief. "I got you, buddy," I told him, lifting his head above the surface.

The ring of rescuers protected us as I towed Josh back to

shore, but as we got close, a chilling realization settled in—Colin. Where was he? I looked behind me. The ocean had settled back into a smooth, flat surface, except for the chunks of broken surfboards floating away. I didn't see him. I called his name over and over, still holding onto Josh, but he never answered. The unthinkable had happened, and our lives would never be the same again.

with me through triumphs and challenges, but now it was just another piece of a life I no longer felt connected to. My gaze fell upon a photograph set on a shelf filled with at least a half-dozen other photos and souvenirs from my years abroad, and I picked it up. It was of me, Josh, and Colin, arms around each other, laughing and hugging Josh after his big win in Bali. He'd just won his first World Surf Championship, beating Chris Cartier, the three-time and reigning champ from France. We stood shoulder to shoulder, our wet suits partially unzipped, saltwater dripping from our hair. Colin's bright green eyes and mop of ginger hair practically sparkled in the sunlight as he stood with an arm thrown across Josh's shoulder, grinning like he'd just pulled off the biggest prank. Josh was sandwiched in between Colin and me, his brown hair sun-bleached nearly platinum, a carefree smile on his lips, and his deep blue eyes staring directly into the camera. And there I was, next to him, trying to look cool and collected, a goofy smirk on my face. My skin was darker, burnished to deep gold, and my dark hair was much shorter, hanging free just past my shoulder. The photo had been taken five years ago, but we looked so young, so very carefree, and looking at it made me feel weary.

We were more than friends; we were a unit, a perfectly balanced trio. Colin was light-hearted and free-spirited like water. Josh was fiery, competitive, and passionate. My nature was grounding, analytical, and steady. Together, we were invincible in our brand and against the waves, our bond forged in our long friendship and tempered by saltwater and adrenaline. We were kings of the ocean then, and everything seemed possible. Fearless and free. The memory of that day, the sound of the waves, the laughter, and the unspoken understanding between us forced a sad smile from me. It all seemed like a dream now, a dream from which I had rudely awakened. Colin was gone, claimed by the very ocean we all loved. Josh, forever altered, was fighting his own demons. And me, the untouched survivor, fractured on the inside.

I rubbed the thick, titanium frame, tracing its edges with my fingertips as if I could somehow connect the gap between then and now. Once masters of the ocean, the unpredictable tides of fate had scattered us. A pang of guilt and grief twisted in my chest. I should have been able to save both Josh and Colin. We were all out on the water together. I should have been able to save at least one of them from the devastation, but that long moment that I'd sat frozen upon my board, watching in horror, the shark had come and gone, leaving excruciating damage in its wake.

I sighed, long and deeply, as I stared at our smiling, youthful faces, frozen in time. I was sorely reminded of what was gone. Reluctantly, I placed the photograph back on the shelf, feeling the weight of the past as I withdrew my hand and let my gaze rove over the many trophies and awards displayed in a glass case. The trophies glinted mockingly in the fading light, each a bitter reminder of victories and a life I had walked away from. The dozen or more trophies were a stark reminder of my past. The glass enclosure housed a collection of gleaming trophies and medals, each a testament to victories and triumphs on the international pro surfing circuit. I opened the case, the sound of the glass door creaking softly, breaking the heaviness of the room.

I opened the glass door, reached in, and examined the trophies one by one. I let my fingers linger over one particularly impressive trophy, a reminder of a championship that had once meant the world to me. For a brief moment, I allowed myself to be transported back to those days of glory —the adrenaline rush of competition, the exuberant cheers of the crowd, the sheer ecstasy of riding the perfect wave. Its surface is cool and smooth to the touch. First Place. It was the first, but not the last, time that I'd beaten Josh for first place in a major championship challenge. It was also the first time—tangible proof that I had what it took to be a champion, and I think that win marked my stepping out of Josh's shadow. I touched a few more, marring their cool, mirrored plate with my fingerprints. As I touched them, the floodgate of memories opened, and I briefly relived the thrill of competition and camaraderie. Such were the moments that had once defined my existence. The structured routine of training and competing had always given me a clear direction, but now my future stretched out like an empty road, vague, uncharted, and filled with an unsettling stillness.

Quitting the pro surfing circuit had felt like the only viable option in the aftermath of the tragedy. The ocean, which had been my sanctuary, now whispered ghostly reminders of loss and what could have been. In leaving the sport behind, it felt as though I had abandoned a part of myself, and I sometimes questioned whether I'd been too rash and whether or not I had done the right thing. I closed the door of the case and quickly turned away, striding back into the living room.

The Sydney skyline outside the windows glittered, indifferent to the turmoil within me, as real as the crashing waves in my tormented memories. I sighed deeply, the sound seeming to echo from the depths of my soul. A restless energy surged through me, and an idea began to take shape, unformed but as real as the memories that haunted me. Perhaps what I needed was a challenge to my mind and body, possibly one of the simpler pleasures of life that I had enjoyed before my world had become all about surfing.

Years ago, I used to take time off and relax by doing some camping and fishing. Josh and I'd met when we were ten years old while I was fishing in the Amblin' River as it crossed his father's land. He'd startled me as I was trying to unhook the biggest fish I'd caught that day, causing me to lose my grip and watch it flip and flop back into the river. I probably wouldn't have caught it again if he hadn't jumped in the river after it. I smiled. An unspoken decision began to form, and the idea had strong appeal. I couldn't remember the last time I'd been camping or fishing. Suddenly, my spirits began to lift, and I felt a surge of energy that I hadn't felt in all the weeks I'd been home. It seemed that getting out of the condo and into the wilderness and fresh air and leaving behind the ghosts that lingered in every corner of this place was a wonderful idea. No destination. No plans. Just me and the vast Australian landscape. Maybe out in the wild, I could find pieces of the man I used to be, or maybe I'd carve out a new path.

With a newfound resolve, I headed toward my bedroom and grabbed my duffel bag. I tossed in clothes and essentials without much thought. As I carried my bag to the living room, set beside the front door, I saw my surfboard. I reached out and let my hand hover over it for a moment. I had no real intention of doing any surfing. This journey wasn't about the waves, but old habits die hard. I picked it up and carried it with my duffle. At sunrise, I'll hit those less traveled roads and reclaim the parts of me I was afraid I'd left behind.

CHAPTER TWO

I pulled up on the driveway of my sister's house in Paddington.

My truck loaded for the long trip, and I was eager to get started, but I couldn't leave without stopping to see Mom and Lizzie, the two most important people in my life. Though I was thirty-six years old, I felt like a kid caught sneaking back in the house after sneaking out, a feeling I'd been very familiar with while growing up. I'd come over early to catch Lizzie before she left for work, and the three of us sat at the kitchen table, a dish of warm scones that Mum had baked sitting in front of us and nursing mugs of strong coffee. They listened as I explained why I was suddenly taking this trip.

My mother sat to my right, and Lizzie, my sister, sat across from me, watching me as I dusted off the crumbs of my second blueberry scone.

"If you want, I can pack you some food for your trip, son," my mum said, ready to hop out of her chair and start baking.

"No need, Mum. Thank you. They're very good, but I'll be fine. I'll only be gone a few days." I reached over to pat her hand. My mother was still youthful, in her mid-fifties. Her beautiful brown face and long-fingered hands were still smooth, and her long, dark hair had fewer visible strands of silver than my own. Her dark eyes reminded me of a hawk as she fastened them on me. Lizzie, however, appeared resigned. She was an old soul, and a lot of it was probably my fault. Growing up, Mum had worked long hours, sometimes weeks at a time, without a single day off, and Lizzie had been charged with taking care of me. It was not her fault she couldn't do a great job of keeping up with me. I could be as slippery as the fish I loved to catch.

Looking at my sister and me, you might find it hard to believe we were full siblings. In appearance, we are as different as night and day. I favored my mother as strongly as Lizzie favored our father, except for a few differences. She was short, five-two, maybe five-three, which she'd inherited from our mother, while I had inherited my father's height, standing head and shoulders above them both, at six-two.

Our father was a white British citizen, and Lizzie's sandy brown hair with reddish-blonde highlights was similar in color to his, but her's was wild, soft, and curly. She was also very fair, with a sprinkling of freckles and hazel-green eyes. My slender and athletic build is a testament to my love for physical activity, and my skin is a warm brown, lighter than Mum's but darker than my father's. My hair is like Mum's, nearly black and thick and straight, and it has grown so long that I wear it in a braid that hangs down my back, almost to my waist. Over the years, it has become a tactile connection for me to my Mum and our heritage. My nose and lips are thin, and my cheekbones and jaw are sharp and angular, reminiscent of my father's Anglo-Saxon heritage. But the feature that stands out the most is my eyes, which are a stormy gray, a color that neither of my parents has.

And as it is not a feature of Torre Straight Islanders, maybe that and the color of my skin make them so striking, catching most people off guard.

I glanced up to see Lizzie's eyes narrowed on me, and she didn't seem very happy with my plans. I loved these two women deeply. They were the pillars of my life, having seen me through thick and thin and ups and downs, but they had no conception of how broken I felt. I hoped they wouldn't give me a hard time. I needed to embark on this journey to find myself again.

"Are you running away from something, Son?" My mother asked me, her voice sounding exceptionally sad, her islander accent thickly coating her words, though she'd left Torres Strait decades ago. Surprised, I quickly looked up at her.

"No, of course not. I'm just taking some time for myself. The only time I've had to myself in the past three years was wrecked…, well, by the shark attack. I need some time to decompress."

"You believe you're all healed from that ordeal?"

Taking a deep breath, I spoke from the heart, "No, not completely, but that will probably take a lot more time. And I don't want to go into it again right now."

"Can't you stay here with us and clear your head?" Lizzie asked, taking a sip of her coffee. "Can't we help you do what you need to do? I worry about you."

"I know you do. But I'll be fine."

"But you've only just come home after almost a year away."

"You should be used to me being away all the time by now.

Don't worry. I plan to drive up the coast, spend time at the ocean, and maybe do some off-shore fishing. I was thinking of maybe stopping up at Palmer Station. It's been a long time since I've been up there."

"Why would you want to go there?" Mum asked sharply. "Nothing in Palmer Station for any of us."

Lizzie covered her hand with her own, and Mom looked somewhat abashed. We'd lived in Palmer Station in north New South Wales when we were small children, and Mum had had a difficult time there, trying to raise us, two obviously half-white children, with no husband. Everyone who lived in that tiny, rural community knew everyone else. They worked on the surrounding large estates, farms and ranches, as that was the only employment in the area. I was too young to realize how few residents had been kind to her, shunning us because they knew my white father hadn't married my mother. In fact, he'd been married to someone else for years, a British lady with whom he had two older boys. My affinity to Palmer Station was the idyllic childhood I'd had because of Josh and his family. Meeting and befriending Josh the summer when we turned ten years old had given me opportunities and freedoms I never would have had otherwise.

"You're probably right," I conceded. "It was just a thought. This trip is about the journey, not the destination," I grinned at Mom and then Lizzie, parroting one of my sister's favorite axioms. Neither of them seemed amused by my cleverness this time. I shrugged. They had always been a hard audience for my brand of witticism.

"We've seen how much you've been struggling, Sean. We want you to be happy." Lizzie reached across the table to squeeze my hand. It was the closest they'd come to talking about the crux of their concern. I could see the concern in her eyes.

"Seriously, now. How long do you plan to be away?"

I met her gaze with reassurance, "A few days, maybe a week, I dunno, but I promise to keep in touch. I'm sure I'll have mobile service most of the time, but when I don't, I'll find a landline somewhere."

Mom stood, and her gentle hands found my shoulders. She hugged me tightly, then pulled away slightly, looking deep into my eyes. "You take care of yourself, Okay?"

"Yes, of course," I nodded. Mom hugged me again, and Lizzie came over and did the same.

"Don't make me come looking for you, little brother."

"I wouldn't dream of dragging you out into the wilds," I said, laughing. Lizzie screwed her face up at me, slapped me on the shoulder, and walked away, while Mum continued to hover.

"I love you both. I'll be fine and come back with a clear head, I promise. I may even bring you enough fish to fill up the freezer."

"No thanks. We'll pass on the fish," Lizzie said from across the room.

I kissed them on the cheek, and after one last hug, I left the house. Climbing up on the driver's seat of my truck, I closed my eyes and allowed a sensation I hadn't felt in a long while to wash over me. It was like a jolt of electricity, an exhilarating feeling of happiness and freedom. I savored the feeling and intended to make the most of this good fortune. I pulled out of the driveway and headed northeast, straight for M1, the Pacific Highway.

CHAPTER THREE

As I drove north, the Australian countryside spread out ahead of me, a breathtaking tapestry of natural beauty.

The road meandered through a landscape that seemed right off a postcard. The eucalyptus trees stood tall and proud, their silver-green leaves shimmering in the sunlight, perfuming the air with their distinctive scent, a blend of earthiness and the unmistakable aroma of the Australian bush. Gum trees lined the roadside, their twisted trunks and branches casting intriguing shadows on the ground, and among the leaves, colorful parrots and cockatoos flitted about, their vibrant plumage a stark contrast against the green backdrop.

The highway occasionally led me through charming coastal towns with quaint cottages painted in pastel colors. I saw fishing boats on the clear blue waters, the men casting their lines and nets, hoping for a bountiful catch. In the evenings, I would stop in whatever town I was near for dinner, the scent of fried fish and other delicacies on the salty sea breeze churning up a ravenous hunger in my belly.

The coastline of New South Wales, as it wound up towards Queensland, was a wonder to behold, with rugged cliffs and golden beaches that stretched for miles. Crystal clear waves crashed against the shore, inviting surfers to ride their crests, while the deep blue depths of the Pacific Ocean extended to the horizon, a vast expanse of endless possibilities. Occasionally, I would spot kangaroos grazing in open fields, their powerful legs ready to propel them into motion at a moment's notice. These iconic marsupials were far from the cuddly bedtime plushies tucked in with children at night. They were wild and often ferocious when approached in the wilderness, and I made certain to avoid them along the roads.

Once the landscape transitioned from coastal to inland, vast expanses of rolling hills and farmland were revealed. Cattle and sheep grazed lazily in green pastures, and the earthy scent of freshly tilled and fertilized soil filled the air. South of the border of Queensland, a hot shower and soft bed started calling my name, and I decided to find a nice enough hotel or B&B to spend at least one night in. Hoping to find something in the town of Carmichael, the next town six miles down the road. I followed the two-lane State Road that split off from the interstate. It seemed as if it had been cut right along the bottom of the rocky cliffs, weathered by time and the relentless ocean. At times, I could see the ocean from the road. The rhythmic rolling of the waves, one after the other, towards the shore and the foamy white spray into the air was hypnotic and soothing. The azure blue water curled and crashed against wind-carved stacks, some twice as tall as a man. It was also a beautiful, mesmerizing spectacle.

I soon saw a sign announcing I was entering the township of Carmichael, population 8,222. Thankful, because I was hungry and needed a pit stop, I took the road that turned away from the edge of the ocean. I rolled down the window, hoping for a fresh, cool breeze. Continuing down High Street towards the town square, I could see it was a busy little community, with people bustling in and out of the quaint little shops and knots of pedestrian traffic heading off in the direction I presumed was toward the beach.

It also looked like Christmas had thrown up over town. Twinkling fairy lights twisted in tinsel and garland had been draped around store windows and entwined in planters and baskets of blooming bougainvillea and fragrant Star Jasmine hanging from the lampposts. I shook my head. There hadn't been this much Christmas merriment across the entire city of Sydney.

Santa Claus, his sleigh pulled by Rudolph and the other happy reindeer, big plastic candy canes, big, colorful holiday ornaments, and twinkling multicolored lights were everywhere.

"Jeez, you've gotta be kidding me," I muttered.

A life-sized plastic Santa hanging ten on a surfboard stood outside a pub, his sunglasses perched jauntily on his jolly red nose, his white cottony beard fluttering in the warm breeze like it was about to take flight. I almost laughed. Almost.

Across the street, there was a display of kangaroos pulling an ancient, rusty Subaru Ute with rear-facing, plastic jump seats decked out like Santa's sleigh, complete with tinsel and a sack of gift-wrapped boxes. The bloody kangaroos had red and green bandanas around their necks, and the life-sized Santa had on a vivid Hawaiian shirt. I squinted and rubbed my temples.

On the corner, in front of a bakery with its windows steamed up, ruining the fake snow and lettering sprayed on them, stood a three-foot Santa with an umbrella drink in one hand, sunglasses, board shorts, and rubber thongs on his feet, welcoming patrons inside. He was grinning like he was on vacation in bloody Bali or something.

When I saw a parking space big enough for my truck, I swerved into it, cut the engine and got out, taking a second to look around. It was late afternoon but still sunny and bright. A large, neat sign announcing *Lily's Cafe and Inn* hanging over the door of a Victorian building in the middle of the block of shops caught my eye, and I strode towards it. Before I'd walked more than halfway there, however, I was sweating balls. My shirt was clinging to my skin, soaking up the sweat trickling down my back and abdomen and from my armpits down my sides. My jeans began to feel like a second skin. It was so damned hot it had to be in the triple digits, and I felt like I'd entered another dimension, one where there were only fake, vacationing Santas relaxing in this unseasonable, unreasonable heat and smiling away like there was no such thing as global warming.

Thank God, I thought as I pushed open the door of Lily's Café and Inn and stepped into the frigid air conditioning and the delicious aromas of roasting meat, baked fruit pies, and freshly brewed coffee. Also, thankfully, there were no plastic, kitschy Santas or twinkling lights. I felt like I'd been delivered to heaven. Lily, the grandmotherly proprietor, greeted me with a friendly smile. Her silver hair framed a handsome face that radiated warmth and good cheer.

"Good afternoon, dear," she said, smiling. "How can I help you?"

I returned her smile, luxuriating in the cool air. "Good afternoon. Do you have any rooms available, maybe for a night or two? And whatever you're serving for dinner tonight smells delicious."

Lily nodded, her smile never wavering. "I think I might have a nice, cozy suite available. And if you're ready to eat, you can go right through to the dining room, rest your bones and feed your belly while I get it ready for you. Where's your car? I suppose you drove into town."

"The next block down. I left it in a parking spot in front of the stores."

"Well, you can park it when you're ready in the lot behind us. It's for my guests."

That sounded wonderful, and I gave her my information and credit card. She told me to stop back by for my key when I finished dining.

"Good evening, Jack. How're you doing?" she asked an elderly gentleman who'd come in behind me.

"Doing better than ever, Lily. Still hot as blazes out there. I thought I'd come here to get something to eat, but mostly to cool off. And good afternoon to you too, young man."

"Hello, Sir," I responded. We walked into the dining room more or less at the same time, and I moved aside, taking a moment to decide where to sit. He tipped his head at me and pointed to a table next to a front window looking out on the street. Tinted, reflective shades were drawn to block the bright afternoon sunlight.

"Would you care to share a table?"

"I don't want to impose on your dinner," I said, looking around at the many empty tables in the room.

"Nonsense. But if you'd rather eat alone, no offense."

"No, no. It's fine. We can share."

"Emmie, Bring…what's your name again?" he asked, leaning toward me to hear.

"Sean, Sir. Sean Hargrove."

"Emmie, hand my new friend, Mr. Hargrove, a menu. I'll have the special." We walked to the table he'd pointed out, him leading and me following, and as we settled in our seats, he asked, "You come for the Big Wave competition that's coming up in a couple of months?"

"No. I haven't heard about it."

"Lots of young folk coming in from all around to surf the big waves on the north end. There's a natural, exposed point break out there that gives nice, big, consistent waves, and at the end of summer, they get even bigger and more powerful. Some promoters came here sometime back and signed with the town council to hold this competition. You might want to come back through for it if you can. It's supposed to be interesting.

"Yessir, it sounds interesting," I answered, perusing the menu.

"None of this Sir nonsense. Call me Jack. Do you know

about surfing?"

"A little, but not about putting on a surfing event."

"Other towns a little further up and down the coast have held this contest, but this will be our first year. Makes a lot of money for the town, from what I hear."

"Yeah, maybe I will stop back through. This is a really nice town, and from what I saw coming from the highway, you have a beautiful spot on the ocean. But besides surfing, what else can I look forward to seeing here? Any good fishing?"

Jack's eyes lit up as he began regaling me with stories about places around town and some of their history. He spoke of hidden waterfalls deep in the nearby forest, a picturesque lighthouse perched on a cliff, and a secret beach known only to the locals. Emmie came over for my order and asked if I wanted something to drink while I waited. Jack ordered a pitcher of summer ale for both of us.

I enjoyed listening to Jack's stories and had a nice buzz going from the three pitchers of ale we'd downed with our delicious meal. I paid for our meals and left Jack downstairs a couple of hours later. I retrieved my truck and parked it in the lot behind the Inn. I then found my room, which was very spacious, clean, and nicely decorated. After a refreshing shower, I hit the sack and was out for the rest of the evening.

CHAPTER
FOUR

The next morning, I ate a hearty breakfast in the dining room as soon as it opened and secured my room for a couple more nights. I then went out to explore the village.

Over dinner the night before, Jack had given me quite a list of things to do and see in and around town, and I was also curious about the Big Wave competition coming to town at the end of summer. I was in no hurry to move on. I had no set destination in mind, and Carmichael was probably as interesting as I was likely to find further up the coast. I took a narrow trail down to the ocean, bypassing the boardwalk that stretched north to the fishing docks and the pier. I walked past the tiny shops that lined it, none of which had yet opened for the day.

The view of the beach was indeed as beautiful as I thought it would be. I could see golden sand, towering palms that swayed in the breeze, and craggy bluffs that extended in both directions, protecting the winding shoreline. It was idyllic. Surfers had come out early to catch the powerful morning tide, and a small group of hot-doggers caught my eye. I watched them for a bit, noticing a couple were putting on quite a show with their acrobatics. They were pretty good, having developed their skill over years of surfing.

I moved on, walking towards the north end of the beach,

where parts of the cliffs had crumbled, leaving giant boulders on the beach and several stacks standing in the water. The waves came in more powerfully the further I walked, likely scraping against a deeper bottom and crashing against a natural shelf. I passed the spot where Jack had told me there were hidden caves, but I couldn't pick them out in the irregular rock face.

However, I could see a house nestled in a gentle cavity along the top of a section of a cliff, accessible from the beach by rugged, uneven steps cut directly into the rock. It appeared empty, faded drapery panels flapping in the wind through two windows that must have been broken out or left wide open. Though it looked smaller and in need of some work, it put me in mind of the Crags, Josh's oceanfront retreat. The Crags was a majestic home built on a precipice overlooking the ocean that Josh had purchased some years back. Intrigued, I climbed the steps, holding fast to the handholds also cut into the rock.

It wasn't a difficult climb once I got a closer look, and I practically ran up to the top. The first thing I noticed was the house was much bigger than it looked from below. What looked like the front porch from below was actually a large balcony off the second floor. Beneath it was an even larger stone patio with a lot of old wrought-iron patio furniture rusting in place by the sun and sea mist; their cushions were long gone. There were no stairs to access the balcony, and the French doors that led inside from the ground-floor patio were securely locked.

I went around to the front of the house. The property was overgrown with towering weeds and fat, prickly bushes. Still,

I could tell there had once been large gardens on either side of the house and a private driveway that ended at the edge of a side building. This later garage addition needed as much or more TLC than the house. The paint was cracked and peeling on every surface.

The place was indeed empty and neglected and apparently had been so for a long time. The once charming façade was now a patchwork of many coats of paint, most of which were different colors. The wooden trim had weathered years of neglect, and wide plank steps, sagging in the middle, were worn smooth by countless footsteps. A faded, plastic *For Sale* sign that had once been tacked on the door hung haphazardly from a single nail. Nothing about the simple, two-story frame with its covered porch was majestic. In fact, it looked like a relic from another era, but the location was perfect.

Cautiously, I climbed the stairs, the creaking floorboards springy and creaking alarmingly underfoot. A narrow porch swing on one end, overlooking the overgrown front yard, swayed gently in the breeze. The rusty chains sounded like nails scraping against a chalkboard and had me grinding my back teeth.

Peering through more broken, grimy windows on the main floor, I could see that the heavy drapery had been pulled down and tossed to the floor. The wallpaper, once a vibrant floral, was faded, peeling, and hanging off the walls in strips, and furniture had been pushed together and covered in white sheets, sagging with the weight of years of dust. An ornate chandelier hung precariously from the ceiling. It looked like a world frozen in time.

Turning around, I squinted out at the fields that seemed to surround the house. There were no other houses nearby, nor could I see any boundary markers. Indeed, if there was as much land attached to the house as I thought there might be, it was absolutely perfect. Fixer-uppers weren't something I was into, and this place needed a lot of fixing up. I wasn't planning to live out here, as I already had two very nice homes and a condo in Sydney. It wouldn't be a good fit for my commercial real estate investments; they were extremely profitable, and this was not. This dilapidated house sat on acres of land in the middle of nowhere and would not improve my portfolio or my net worth. Still, it continued to intrigue me. I knew it could become a jewel—with a generous budget and a lot of work, it could become a nice getaway from the city.

That evening, after finishing my meal, I approached Lily, who seemed to staff the front desk all day, every day.

"Lily," I began, "I saw an old house on top of the cliffs on the far north end of town. It had a sign stating it was for sale tacked to the door, but no information on it. Do you know anything about it or who owns it?"

Lily's eyes crinkled with a knowing smile. "Ah, sure, you're talking about the Henderson place. That old place has been vacant for years. No one will rent it or buy it without the family putting in some TLC. They'd rather see it fall down before parting with a single cent. Paula Cook-Anderson is the real estate agent, and she has an office two blocks down."

My excitement built up in my chest as I leaned in, eager to

know more. "What do you think of the place? Do you think it's worth buying and fixing it up? I thought it might make a nice vacation home once it's habitable again."

"You thinking of buying that old place? I thought you were passing through."

"I am...I mean, I was, but it's perfect for what I have in mind."

"Really?" Lily shook her head, her voice tinged with surprise. "You a real estate developer or something, wanting to buy that old place like that?"

"No, not at all."

"You don't look familiar to me, so I know you didn't grow up here. You connected to this town, somehow?" She scrutinized me like I was about to grow horns or something, and I shook my head.

"Well, you can imagine how strange it seems that you came here for a room and a meal, and now you're thinking about settling down here. You know what I'm saying?"

"Yeah, I know it seems odd. Feels a little odd to me, too, but I needed to get away from the city for a little while, and this little road trip was for me to find a bit of peace and quiet near the ocean."

"That's Carmichael to a T, but the old Henderson place is a project. Nothing will be peaceful or quiet about it. It'll need a lot of work, and that costs money. Ain't many folks 'round here got a surplus of money to sink into a place like that. I haven't been around there in a good while, but it had good bones. It's probably about a hundred years old, and it's been in the Henderson family for generations. Jonas Henderson died two, maybe three years back and left everything to his boy, Garth. When he came home from serving his time in the military, he married a city girl from up near Melbourne and moved up there. When his daddy died, he dumped the family business and put the family home up for sale."

"If it's priced reasonably, I might be interested. I could come here every year and watch the Big Wave competition. It should have a good view."

"You could come and stay at the Inn every year. Bring your family, too."

"Yeah, that's an option."

With a kind and knowing smile that people generally reserved for those who couldn't see reason, no matter how much a person tried to talk sense into them, Lily wrote on a pad of paper the address and handed it to me. "Here you go, dear. Here's Pamela Cook-Anderson's office number. I'm sure she'd be happy to talk with you. If anyone can, I bet you can turn that old sow's ear into a silk purse."

"Thanks, Lily. Maybe I'll have a little conversation with Ms. Cook-Anderson tomorrow."

"It ain't too late right now, and she might still be in her office. Give her a call and set up an appointment for tomorrow."

I looked at her quizzically. "Okay. I guess I will."

I headed up to my room, dialing the number Lily gave me as I jogged up the flight of stairs. A woman answered on the second ring, announcing I'd reached the office of Cook-Anderson Realty. When she asked if she could help me, I asked if I could make an appointment for tomorrow to talk to someone about the Henderson property. She answered, "Certainly," and asked me to "Please hold."

~

I don't remember a real estate deal ever going as smoothly or as quickly as the purchase and closing of the Henderson property. It only took a few days from start to finish, and within the week, I was able to start envisioning the changes I wanted made to the weather-beaten structure inside and out. There was no doubt that it needed work from one end to the other, from the bottom to the top, but I hoped it was structurally sound.

Inside, sunlight streamed through the grimy and broken windows, illuminating the character of each room. It was a diamond in the rough, a canvas ready for a new chapter. The excitement and anticipation of fully renovating it filled my heart, but it was also a little overwhelming. I'd never done any home improvement in my adult life. There was no way I could take on a project this size without help. Lily was a wealth of information, and sometimes, I felt bad for bothering her so much. But with her ever-present and warm smile, she'd spot me hovering uncertainly nearby, waiting to talk to her, and she'd wave me over.

My excitement spilling over, I approached the counter and leaned in close to whisper, "The deal is done, and I bought the

Henderson place."

Lily's eyes sparkled with approval. "Oh, that's wonderful news, dear! That place has been waiting for someone like you. Let me think. I know just the folks who can help." This time, she jotted down some names and numbers on her pad of paper, her handwriting neat and precise. "Here you go, Dear. These are some of the best contractors and artisans in town. They've worked on plenty of renovation projects like this before. And this is the best general contractor in town." I took the list gratefully, feeling a deep sense of gratitude for her advice and support.

"Thank you so much, Lily. I really appreciate your help. I can't wait to get started."

Lily's smile was filled with encouragement. "It's going to be a labor of love, but I have no doubt you'll turn it into something truly special. If you ever need anything else, don't hesitate to ask."

With the precious list of trusted names in hand, I ran up the stairs to my room, eager to get started.

I was out at the house, making a list of things I saw that needed repairing or replacing. The floors had warped with age and some water damage. The furniture, rugs, ruined drapes, and peeling wallpaper had to go, and the kitchen and bathroom were a total gut. But beyond the decay and destruction, I saw potential. I imagined it transformed into a cozy haven, with fresh paint, refinished floors, oversized leather furniture, and a giant TV mounted over the fireplace, a crackling fire inside. I could see it turned into the same warm and inviting space I loved about the Crags. I didn't have much imagination for the overgrown garden or the land beyond it, but the road needed grading and repaving. I didn't want to tear the undercarriage from underneath my car when I drove up here from Sydney for a relaxing weekend.

A loud knock on the front door roused me from my daydreams, and I hurried to answer it. I was pleasantly surprised by a young woman with bright blue eyes, blonde hair pulled into a high ponytail, and dressed in overalls standing in the doorway. She stuck her hand out, and I reciprocated, feeling her firm shake.

"Hi there," she greeted me with a warm smile. "I'm Lara Finnegan. Lily, my grandmother, mentioned you bought this old place and had plans for fixing it up, so I thought I might run over here and take a look around. I'm hoping to become your general contractor."

"Ah, yes. L. Finnegan. She didn't tell me…, ah, that you were going to stop by."

"She probably didn't know. I didn't know until this morning, but I'm assuming she didn't tell you that L. Finnegan was a woman or that I was her granddaughter."

"No, she didn't, but she did say you were the best."

"It makes me blush when she brags about me, but she is right. I am the best."

"Well, come in and look around," I said, looking around the living room, shadows lingering even though the sun was blindingly bright outside, then back to her.

"Thank you. I won't take long."

I moved aside to let her in, leaving the door open and hanging off the hinges to let in some fresh air. "I've got experience working as a general contractor here in town, and I know all of the best tradespeople. I can make sure everything runs smoothly and we get the work done to your satisfaction," she said, nodding confidently, striding past me.

"It looks like everything needs attention."

"It's still sturdy and probably not as bad as you think. But I haven't really been out here since Mr. Jonas died. His son thought it would take too much money to fix up, and he was content living up in Melbourne." She walked away, looking inside the different rooms, checking out corners and cubbies, and jotting things down in a little notebook she carried. When she came back into the living room, I was anxious for her opinion.

"So, what do you think?" I asked her.

"Well, it is going to take some work…and money, but I believe it's doable. Lily said you wanted to make it shine again."

"Okay, yeah. More than just some work, but how much work? Can you give me a ballpark figure on how much money?"

"How much are you willing to spend? I could make this place shine in eight weeks with a sizable budget, or we can clean it up, slap on some paint and hang a new door and windows." I laughed, pleased by her honesty.

"I want it to shine, but I don't know if I want to keep a room at the Inn for eight weeks."

"I can have a new roof on and an upstairs bedroom and en-suite finished in a couple of weeks so that you can move in up there. The rest of the time, we'll be down here, but you can't be walking through, going in and out. I think a temporary set of stairs up to the back deck from the patio so that you can get in and out that way should work."

"Temporary?"

"They'd be sturdy enough, though I wouldn't leave them up permanently unless you wanted them that way."

I nodded thoughtfully. I liked the sound of her plan, and staying on the top floor during the renovation instead of at Lily's inn suited me just fine. I could come and go through the French doors off the back deck and take the rock-face stairway down to the beach or walk around the house to the driveway to get in my truck. Also, it made sense to have someone local with a good reputation in the community onsite, ensuring the work got done and done well.

""Well, Lara Finnegan, I think we have a deal. I'm Sean Hargrove, by the way."

"I know," she said and smiled. We shook hands, and I could see the confidence in her eyes. I couldn't have been happier to accept. I was going to have to get Lily something really nice in appreciation for her help. She was a lifeline, whether she knew it or not.

"Lara, you have no idea how much this helps. I'm excited to get started."

"Me, too. Let me take a look around some more, take some measurements, and see what we're working with." She turned and looked around, writing in her notebook as she thought aloud.

"First thing is to get Stan Pettigrew up on the roof. We can't do much until he's done that. We can't have rain undoing all of our work inside. Maybe Fred Jolly's free to come and start stripping the floors and sanding them even," she said, talking aloud to herself and not me.

Leaving her to make her plans, I stepped outside, but it didn't take long for her to go through the house and finish her notes. She came from around the side, having gone out through the kitchen door which led to the side yard. I was sitting on the top step of the front porch, and I smiled back at her as she climbed the steps to sit next to me, her list of improvements in hand.

"I think it may take about ten weeks to do everything that I see. But that's to ensure it's solid from the foundation to the roof."

"I think we need to pave that road too."

"The road?"

"Yeah. I have expensive cars, and I don't want them jacked up on that pitiful excuse of a road."

"I can get you a quote for that."

"Fine." She added the road to her list of improvements.

We sat together a little longer, and I added more things to her list. When we had everything I could think of on the list, she gave me a look that made me wonder if I had lost my mind.

"You know this will all be extremely expensive. The road alone…."

"I know," I said, "but it'll be worth it, especially if you can get the work done a lot quicker than ten weeks."

She balked for a moment. "I'd have to practically double the number of workers to get it done any faster."

"Okay," I said. It wasn't like I was asking for a lot of structural changes or adding to the footprint. And I didn't have to stay in Carmichael the entire time. The purpose of the trip had been to do a little camping, maybe some fishing, which I could still do, and I could come and check on the progress of the renovation here and there. We shook on the deal, and she promised to have a contract ready for my signature the next day.

CHAPTER
FIVE

Though I had planned to go off the grid, even after purchasing the Henderson property, the need no longer felt as pressing as before.

Instead, I became more interested in helping as much as my limited skills allowed with the renovation. I outfitted myself in jeans, long-sleeved t-shirts, work boots and thick gloves to protect myself from insects, little work hazards, and sunburn, and drove to the project from my room at the Inn every morning. The first day, Lara loaned me a well-worn tool belt and a few tools that were almost completely useless in my hands. Then, I gathered in the front yard with her work crew and sipped hot coffee from a thermos while she assigned the day's duties. I was given some practical, unskilled tasks, like sweeping up, helping with a little touch-up sanding and painting, tacking wood trim, and helping the guys when they needed to move heavy or awkward or both heavy and awkward things. The physical labor was a welcome distraction, providing a sense of purpose and accomplishment that helped keep my mind focused and occupied. I felt less anxious and melancholy than I had in months.

By the third week, the new roof and interior of the second floor were completed, efficiency windows were installed, and I was allowed to move into the second floor. Work ramped up on the main floor, and the crews were able to focus on finishing the rooms in record time. In the evenings, when the sun began its descent over the ocean and everyone had left for home, I would go around to the back of the house and climb my stairs to heaven. I'd clean up, get dressed in loose cargo shorts and a clean T-shirt, and go down to the diner for dinner. Before bed, I'd sit out on the balcony and listen to the waves crashing on the shore and feel the wind rustling through the leaves and the soft cooing of the birds nesting in the nearby trees. Sometimes, I would meditate, acknowledging the pain and guilt that still lingered, but also give thanks for the new lease on life that was slowly taking hold. Other times, I would let the night soothe me, and afterward, I would sleep like a baby.

Time flew by quickly. I'd arrived In Carmichael over a month ago and had been staying in the house for the past two weeks. And the house was coming along. Lara still wouldn't let me walk through the main floor, and with the upstairs complete and little to do on the exterior, I was left to my own devices. I started taking my board out in the mornings and spending a couple of hours on the water, keeping mostly to myself, as I wasn't ready for people to know who I was. I didn't want to be treated like a celebrity, which usually happened when Josh, Colin, and I would try to train, and people recognized us, especially surf fans who followed the circuits on social media.

One morning, I'd been out surfing, and as I returned to the house, I saw Lara standing in the new garden. I unhooked my board that was strapped to my back and set it and the harness that I'd cobbled together so that I could easily carry it up and down the rock-face stairway when I felt like doing a little surfing and placed the board and leather strapping on the rack against the house.

"Come see, Sean. The house is turning out amazing," she said as soon as I stepped around the side of the house.

I'd picked up my towel from where I'd left it on the patio to blot the remaining water from my skin and hair and slipped on my shoes. Continuing to wipe off as much dripping seawater as I could, I followed Lara through the front door of the house. It was the first time I'd been inside in weeks.

"Isn't it absolutely gorgeous?" She practically twirled around. It was a hive of activity, and I could hardly believe the transformation that had taken place in a couple of weeks. No longer needing a split crew, one to work on the upstairs, the other to work downstairs, Lara had focused their full attention on reconfiguring and renovating the entire interior of the main floor. The rooms had shed their weathered, neglected air, and I followed along as she pointed out the changes, excitement evident in her voice.

"So what do you think?"

"You're right. It is amazing."

"We've made so much progress these last two weeks. We've stripped away all of the old wallpaper, replastered the walls, and refinished the floors. We opened that wall for you, giving you a direct connection to the kitchen and new dining room. It's a more open and airy space now."

The living room, once dim and dusty, was now bathed in natural light, thanks to the newly hung windows, still uncovered by blinds or drapery. The old hardwood floors gleamed with a fresh, dark finish, and the old fireplace had been revitalized as the centerpiece of the room.

"We're also working on the kitchen. It's getting a complete overhaul with a better layout, cabinets, counters and appliances. And we've added a large window to give you a view of the garden while you cook."

I couldn't help but smile, seeing everything take shape. "It's incredible. It looks almost finished." Lara's eyes sparkled with pride. "I think we'll make that six-week deadline. Have you decided on the furniture?"

"Yes, and the order's been placed."

"Awesome. I've got the landscapers clearing out the gardens, and it's going to be a lovely outdoor space for you."

As we stepped outside, I could see the transformation underway. The overgrown garden had been tamed, hidden paths and potential spaces for relaxation had been revealed, and the proposed new covered deck on the north side of the building would provide the perfect spot to enjoy the outdoors. I couldn't have been more grateful for Lara's expertise and dedication. The old house was well on its way to becoming the serene and rejuvenating retreat I had envisioned. It was well worth the bonus I was paying to get it completed quicker.

She climbed the new steps onto the brand-new porch and sat down on the new porch swing. I sat down beside her. It had been oriented to look out and away from the house, and I marveled at the work crew tackling the road leading up to the property.

"So? How about that?" she asked, seeing that I'd noticed the new project.

"You're a miracle worker."

"An expensive road for expensive cars," she said, grinning and staring at the workers.

"What can I say? I am a man of discriminating taste."

"So I see." She nodded, looking back at me, her eyes shining with pride. "I'm glad you're happy with everything. It's been a great project, and I wanted you to see the amount of progress we've made in weeks. You've been the perfect client, mostly because you like every suggestion I make and don't flinch at the price tag."

I nodded. "I do, don't I? And I do flinch at the price tags, though mostly when I check the bank balance."

She laughed happily. As I looked at her, sitting beside me, the breeze teasing her ponytail, and one booted foot kicking off against the floor, making the swing sway back and forth, an unexpected feeling began to stir within me. It was more than gratitude for her expertise; it was more of a growing attraction. Her confidence, her passion for and dedication to my renovation project were undeniably appealing, but there was more to it. I found myself watching the way she talked about the project, her hands gesturing as she described the next steps.

However, the more I watched her, it seemed her focus was entirely on the house and the work at hand. There was no hint of a reciprocal attraction in her gaze when she looked back at me, and her smiles were friendly, not flirtatious or seductive. I tried to dismiss my feelings, telling myself that it was just a fleeting attraction, a byproduct of the time we were spending together. Maybe that in itself was so attractive about her. I needed to get myself together, stop thinking about her in that way, and focus on what she was saying. We went through plans for the remaining work, and she looked over the invoices for the furnishings she had me order.

"I'll check with these companies and confirm shipping. I want to make sure they'll be here on time, and I can schedule Marie and her team to come and put it all together." She stopped the swing and hopped off. "It's back to work for me. I'm so glad you like everything so far."

I also stood up, tossing the damp towel I'd been carrying and had used to sit on around my neck.

"I love it. Thanks for giving me an update."

She went inside through the front door, and I went down the steps and around to the patio. My stomach was growling, and unless I missed my guess, they were serving lunch right about now at Lily's.

As the days passed, I found liked being in the old house, even if I was constrained to the second floor. I would wake up to the sun coming up over the ocean and the gulls circling at eye level as they scoured the beach for breakfast. I couldn't make coffee in my room, but I had an electric kettle for tea, and sometimes, I'd drink it outside. It was much cooler, with the breeze blowing in off the ocean, and the sound of the waves sometimes muted the construction noise going on downstairs.

One morning, I'm leaning on the deck railing, soaking in the ocean's endless blues. My eyes catch a ripple way out in the deep water. Dolphins? Whales? I squint to get a better look.

And then, boom, my heart's in my throat. A tiny voice in my head tries to calm me down, "Just animals, Sean. Chill." But nope, my lungs don't get the memo; air gets scarce. Everything blurs, and I grip the railing so tight my knuckles go ghost-white. Suddenly, I'm spiraling back into a memory I tried to bury, but here it is, resurfacing like a cork in water.

I'm back there. Josh is in the water, paddle racing with Colin. Josh gets launched into the air by—oh God—a great white. There's red in the water, and my heart's jammed in my throat again. I'm paddling through the blood-tinged surf, desperate, panicked. I reach him; he's alive but torn up. "I got you," I remember saying, my voice shaky as hell. I blink. Where's Colin? All I see are pieces of smashed surfboards floating like the shattered bits of my past.

Then, in a flash, Colin's there, his voice so vivid it's like a punch to my gut. "Race you to that buoy and back, Sean," he's saying, his laughter echoing in my ears like some twisted soundtrack to my nightmare. I'm swimming, but it's like moving through molasses, and every stroke takes forever. I'm not fast enough. I'll never be fast enough.

A scream ripped through the fog in my head, and I snapped back to the present, my hands still vice-gripping the railing. The ocean is just the ocean again, the surfers still surfing, and the dolphins or whales or whatever they were, are gone. My legs are Jell-O, and I let go of the railing. I exhaled, feeling shaky, like I was deflating, and shook my head, trying to clear my thoughts. *I should've done something* played on a loop in my brain, and I whispered those four words aloud, feeling them scrape raw against my chest and throat, rising from somewhere deep within me. *I should've done something!* Should've done what? What could I have done against a primal force of nature? What chance did I have? Still, the guilt pulled me down like an anchor.

I turn around and go back inside, closing the door behind me. I see the bottle of water I left on the windowsill and grab it, swallowing down the tepid water inside. My mind is reeling, torn between the here and now and a past that refused to stay buried, and I feel like I've been run over. The water doesn't make me feel any better. I'll probably need something stronger for that to happen.

I inhale and exhale long, deep breaths. I know that I have been running from myself since that day. I know that I have not faced myself or the truth of what I felt as I sat on my board and watched that tragedy play out in front of me. The fact that I was frozen in fear is a reality that I cannot deny, even to myself. For long seconds, I could not believe what I saw, and then I could not act. I didn't know what to do at first. Had I acted sooner, maybe I could have reached Colin, and together, we could have reached Josh. Could've. Should've. It was too late to change the past, but it plays on a loop in my brain anyway.

Someday, I'll have to reclaim the piece of myself that I left out there in the ocean. I'll have to get mentally stronger to go back for it, to reconcile—if not absolve myself—of the guilt I feel for not being able to save my friends. I did all that I could, and I can't let my doubts and fears continue to weaken me. Josh is getting the help he needs to overcome his mental and physical scars, but I'm not ready for that. I'll try it my way, at least for a while. I have enough to focus on right now, a lot to keep my mind busy.

CHAPTER
SIX

I was helping Lloyd McCarren unload his truckload of two-by-fours, four-by-sixes, and other framing materials in the drive-way when Lara pulled up in her battered work SUV behind him.

I nodded to her as we carried the materials to the porch and piled them up. Lloyd went inside to get more help, and I came off the steps to meet her. My attraction to Lara not only seemed to linger, but because I was now acutely aware of her, it was becoming stronger. It was a confusing mix of emotions for me.

On the one hand, I was grateful for her presence and the renewed sense of purpose she had brought to my life, but on the other hand, I was wrestling with feelings that seemed to have no place in our professional partnership. Women were no mystery to me, and I'd shared the company of beautiful women all over the world. Most times, they approached me rather than the other way around. But I don't fall in love. Josh and I and some of the members of our team used to tease Colin unmercifully about his habit of falling in love at the bat of an eyelash. He said he never broke up with them, but instead, he let them go like the pretty butterflies they were.

I believed he loved being in love. I, on the other hand, made sure my partner and I both enjoyed our time together. No strings. No clinging. No messy endings. Maybe I needed to return to

Sydney for a couple of weeks until the house was complete and call up a few friends. I'd been celibate for a while, my mind preoccupied with other things. But just as quickly as the thought came to me, I dismissed it. That would be worse than dealing with my unprofessional attraction to Lara. She wasn't interested in me, and that cooled my ardor considerably.

We talked for a few minutes, mostly about the progress of the work, and seeing Lloyd come back outside with a few helpers, we said goodbye, and I set about moving more materials. A few days later, the entire crew and I were out on the stone patio, feasting on a huge lunch Lily had sent over. The group was in a good mood, laughing and joking around with each other, when one of the carpenters, a man several years younger than I, called over to me.

"So, Sean, I've seen you out there on your board," he said, pointing the can of soda he held in his hand toward the ocean. "You going to compete in the Big Wave competition?"

"No, but I plan to watch from this perfect vantage point."

"You should think about it. I think you could take top honors. I've been watching you sometimes. Out early in the morning. You're pretty good."

"Thank you, but I don't think so." I smiled, hoping he'd drop it, but it seemed his comment started a conversation on the topic.

"Lots of young people coming to compete, but we've got some local boys that will raise the bar. Cal Eaton is a shoo-in for first place. Never seen anyone like him on a surfboard. Not even his uncle, John Marsh, though he taught Cal everything he knows."

"Johnny could've been as good as those boys that took over the National and International circuits some years back. Rumored they came from a small town up this way. Had a famous surfer train them too."

The conversation was getting a little too close to home, and I turned to Lara. "Are you and your crews involved in the building of the spectator stands going up on the beach."

Lara chuckled. "Not even remotely involved. I totally disagree with the way Rubin Loftus throws them up all over the place, but I don't have a say so with the town council. Anyway, the competition will put Carmichael on the map, especially with it coming back year after year. It was up in Spenser for three years, and before that, it was in Mercy. Both towns have been growing by leaps and bounds."

"Well, that means it's going to be good for this town too."

"Maybe, but we don't have a lot of places for so many people, both surfers and tourists, to stay. They'll be flooding into town, and there's just no room for them all. You know there's no excess lodging here. You probably bought one of the few houses on the market. The town council didn't want to go through the efforts of begging up enough money to put up new tract housing that could be rented out. I don't know if there is even enough money available without outside funding."

I furrowed my brow, sensing some tension in her tone. "Well, where are all those people going to stay? Lily's Inn and the B&B I saw probably wouldn't be able to accommodate more than a dozen large families combined."

Lara explained, "Well, the surfers will likely stay in their tents, trailers, vans, cars, and RVs, anywhere they can. Some will have to camp out by the interstate. It'll be close enough for them to get back and forth. They can practice and get familiar with the waves before the competition. Fans, families, and tourists will probably come in their campers and spread out around them. I expect some of them might come up this far and want to spread out in your fields, if not further. Some of the residents aren't too thrilled about the crowd, noise, and trash or the contract with producers the council signed for the next three years. They worry it might change the character of our town. It's a big debate among residents."

I could understand their concerns. Having been here a few weeks, I've learned that Carmichael is a quiet community, and the sudden influx of visitors and the buzz around the competition could disrupt the tranquil atmosphere.

"So, the council's doing nothing to address these concerns?" I asked.

Lara shook her head. "The town council is trying to strike a balance. They want to support the competition, feeling it's a big opportunity for Carmichael, but they also have to answer to the residents' demands for peace and well-being. And, there's the fact we don't have a lot of money. The money the producer gave them as a guarantee is being used for spectator stands, portable loos, hiring security, and things like that. It's a delicate balance."

"There's not much time, either. There's what, two months left?"

"There was time, but they've been bickering and dickering about for over a year. My Grandma's prepared to feed an army three meals a day, but as far as I know, she's the only one with that much foresight."

Suddenly, Lara turned and looked at me, "You looked familiar to me when we first met, but I couldn't place you. But listening to Bert a minute ago, it's coming back to me. Your name… you used to surf professionally, didn't you?"

I leaned back in my chair, gazing out at the horizon as memories of my surfing days flooded my mind. "Yeah, you could say so."

Suddenly, her eyes widened with realization, and her gaze seemed to search my face for confirmation. A hint of a smile played at the corners of her lips as she connected the dots. "Sean Hargrove, Sean Hargrove, she repeated. They're talking about you, aren't they? You're that famous champion surfer Bert's talking about, right?"

I chuckled nervously, heat creeping onto my face. It wasn't something I talked about often these days. "Well, yeah, that's who I was."

Lara's excitement was palpable. "I've seen you and your buddies' photos and read about your legendary surf careers in magazines. You guys are like legends."

I couldn't help but feel a mix of embarrassment and nostalgia. "It feels like a lifetime ago now. I've moved on from the competitive scene. I'm just a regular guy now." I put my finger up to my lips.

"No way. My God, that must have been incredible. What was it like winning championships and flying all over the world?" she asked, lowering her voice to a whisper.

I took a moment to collect my thoughts before responding. "It was incredible. My family was poor, and I met Josh when we were about ten years old. His family is wealthy…"

"Got more money than God, is what I heard."

"I suppose, but Josh was just a kid and my friend. We got into surfing when we met Colin and his uncle Charlie. Charlie Miele used to be a champion surfer but broke his back in an accident and had to retire. Surfing, at least for me, was more than just a sport. It became my way out of poverty, my family's way out, and gave us a very good life."

"I don't surf, don't have the flexibility for it, but I see the guys out there. What was it like surfing for thousands of people and being on television?"

"I didn't perform for the crowds like that. For me, it's always been like dancing with the sea. The feeling of catching a wave, riding it with the ocean's power beneath you—it's hard to put into words." I closed my eyes briefly as if reliving those moments. "There's a connection that you develop with the ocean, and it becomes a part of who you are. It's freedom and exhilaration all rolled into one."

Her questions had the power to transport me back to a time I didn't want to revisit, so I concentrated on memories of times when I was one with the sea. I leaned forward, my eyes distant as I began to describe those exhilarating moments on the water.

"There's magic to it, you know?" I said after a moment. "The early morning surf sessions, when the sun's just rising, and you're out there, alone, waiting for that perfect wave. The anticipation is electric."

I looked at her, and she was staring at me, bemused. I continued, sitting forward in my seat. "You paddle out, past the breakers, feeling the rhythm of the ocean beneath you, the saltwater spray on your skin. And you wait. You wait until you feel the water building and surging beneath you like the ocean is getting ready to play with you. Then you see it. You only have a second before it's coming at you, and when it comes, it's like a force of nature. You paddle hard, feel it lift you, and then you're up, riding the face. Time slows down, and it's just you, the board, and the ocean. You carve turns, feeling the board respond to your every movement. And the sound of it is louder than a motor raceway, a roar you feel all the way to your bones, that's both exhilarating and humbling."

Lara's eyes were wide, caught up in the imagery of it. "It sounds incredible, Sean. I can almost picture it."

I nodded, the memories washing over me like a wave. "It was incredible. My best friends and I rode our wave to the top of the game. Josh Brenner, Sean Hargrove, and Colin Mitchel—the triple threat. Josh and I are retired now, and I plan to enjoy the sport from the shore."

I looked over at her; her enthusiasm and excitement were clearly reflected in her face. I didn't want her to look at me differently. I didn't want her looking at me with star-dazed eyes.

"I remember reading about the shark attack. All the news outlets carried the story, and you guys kinda dropped out of sight."

I let out a sigh, my gaze returning to the garden. "Yeah. Then you know Colin died, and Josh had been critically injured. He'll never surf again and has lost his affinity for the ocean. For me, competing paled in comparison to that. I haven't lost my love for the ocean or for surfing, but I don't have it in me to compete anymore."

Lara nodded, her expression thoughtful. "Perhaps it'll come back someday. Especially since it used to mean so much to you. Maybe this Big Wave competition will help bring a bit of that spirit back into your life."

"Perhaps," I chuckled, a mixture of nostalgia and resignation in my voice.

I remained out on the patio after the workers had gone back inside the house. I was feeling restless after sharing my story with Lara like the calm and peacefulness I'd slipped into had been shattered. She now knew who I was, and though I hadn't explicitly been trying to hide my identity, it had felt good to be anonymous around town. The workers might even start putting two and two together, and then anonymity would be impossible to recapture.

The next morning, I made my way over to the Inn for a to-go cup of coffee before another day of work began on the house. I also noticed more shiny new cars, SUVs, trucks and RVs parked on the street and in the lot behind the Inn.

It seemed that, overnight, droves of people had arrived in town without fanfare, though my place was a little far for me to catch the fanfare if it had happened. I could hear the indistinct sound of loud voices and cheering coming from the direction of the beach, and I knew the surfers, their fans and hangers-on, and possibly media trucks were beginning to descend on the little town. I decided to take my coffee down to the beach, curious to see how many competitors were on the water and if I knew anyone out there.

The morning sun was beginning to break through the cloud cover, casting a bright, golden hue over the coastline, and the rhythmic sound of the waves called to me like an old friend. The streets circumventing High Street were quiet, the boardwalk out onto the sandy beach was empty, and the flocks of seagulls squawked overhead, their wings catching the warm breeze that brought in a salty tang from the ocean.

Waves rolled towards the shore, slammed into the shelf hidden just below the surface, and exploded into frothy spray sent up at least three feet high. An obvious tourist and hobbyist angler, fashionably outfitted in Patagonia labels from head to toe and standing in hip boots in the surf, tried his hand at catching something Instagram-worthy. I grinned, thinking he'd never catch anything more than long strands of kelpy seaweed unless he went out on a fishing charter or fished off the pier.

I continued walking further down the beach, lulled by the gentle breeze ruffling the fronds of towering palm trees and the sound of the crashing waves, and as I rounded an outcropping of rock at the bottom of the bluff that was taller than my height of six-four, I came upon a crowd buzzing with anticipation, gathered along the water's edge. My eyes tracked their gaze, and I saw dozens of surfers bobbing on their boards like sleek fish waiting for the perfect wave. I was surprised as there'd been nothing to prepare me for such a crowd.

The first set of waves rolled in, and surfers paddled furiously, their muscles rippling beneath sun-kissed skin, and a collective cheer erupted from the onlookers. Like synchronized dancing, the surfers caught the waves, and the ocean seemed to curl and dip in concert with the rider.

I noticed a surfer executing daring tricks, launching into the air and spinning his board beneath him. The crowd cheered and clapped; their excitement was infectious. But then I saw a teenage boy, probably no older than eighteen or nineteen, riding a wave with effortless grace, carving smooth lines as if he was, in fact, dancing on water. It was like watching a mythical merman, a fish that had been given human form. His dark hair flowed behind him, his locks snapping in the wind, his bronzed skin gleaming in the sunshine. But it wasn't just his looks; it was the way he moved on that board. Effortless. Fluid. Like the ocean was a part of him. I smiled as I anticipated his next moves. It seemed he never tired.

When a monstrous wave approached, the other surfers paddled furiously to escape its wrath, but this boy headed straight for it, sliding up the side and standing tall atop it, his silhouette in sharp relief against the bright and vivid and laser-sharp morning sky. I climbed up on a boulder, aiming to see over the heads of the crowd standing around for a better view. And then, just when I thought he'd be consumed by the wave, he turned his board sharply, cutting across the face, riding it with an effortlessness that left me awe-struck. Damn, who is this kid? I wondered. His every move was a testament to his mastery. When the wave curled, he seemed to whisper secrets to it, urging it to let him ride its most hidden corners. It was like he knew the water, understanding it in ways that I was sure he was too young to know about. Intense admiration hit me. He was good. Damn good, and I wanted to know his story and who had trained him to make art on water.

As he rode the wave until it broke, splashes of foam trailing him, I could see his dark eyes, bright and alive, with unbridled joy on his face and that brand of fire that was contagious. Even from this distance, it warmed something deep inside me, reminding me of myself, Josh and Colin out on our boards, at his age, learning and training under Charlie's meticulous eye. Life for us had been all about surfing back then, and we'd been lucky. Under Charlie's tutelage, we'd become elite in the sport, winning international competitions and earning lucrative purses that accompanied world titles. It had been a good life for three global nomads who'd put off adulthood and responsibility for as long as they could. This boy could take our places. There was a void at the top, and he could probably step right in our shoes.

I don't know how long I sat there watching and enjoying myself, but the sun became too bright and too warm to sit any longer. Besides, the crew was probably already at the house, and work had started. I needed to hurry along if I didn't want Lara to think I was lollygagging.

I went back to the beach that evening and the next morning, hoping to see the boy surf again and get his name at least. I wanted to ask him about his plans for the Big Wave contest coming to town in a few weeks and ask his permission to talk to a few friends who might be interested in coming down to see him perform. However, it seemed he'd disappeared.

~

As I made my way down the sandy path, I couldn't help but feel a sense of hope and anticipation. I could hear the crowd on the beach before I even approached the outcrop, and I instinctively knew he was out on the water. I was in time to catch the waves beginning to rumble, an eternal orchestra of the ocean, and the boy paddling out with a rhythm that bespoke countless hours in the water. His long, sinewy arms dipped in and out of the sea with the grace of a seasoned oarsman, water droplets racing down the lean contours of his muscles. His board, a sleek expanse of bright yellow with streaks of black, slid through the water with him on top. It seemed an extension of the boy himself as if the two had fused into one entity over time. I could see his toes peek out from the water now and then, beyond the board's edge, subtly adjusting and guiding its path. Those brown feet, weathered and calloused, told tales of sandy beaches and rocky shores, and the movements were familiar to me. My own feet began to mimic his.

Beneath him, the water was a kaleidoscope of colors - deep shades of blues and greens intermingled with the translucent shallows, the surface ruffling with every breeze. He positioned himself, waiting for the perfect wave, and then, as a promising swell approached, there was a brief moment of stillness. The boy coiled like a spring, every muscle taut, every sense alert. It was the quiet before the storm, a fleeting second of anticipation before the dance began once again.

I jumped up, caught up in the excitement, cheering with the crowd. It was a masterful, exhilarating ride. I slid off the boulder and trod across the sand to be at the water's edge when the boy came ashore. I hesitated for a moment, watching as he glided to the shore, water running off him in rivulets. Gathering my excitement, I walked toward the water's edge, my footprints merging with the wet sand.

"Hey," I called out, trying to sound casual but feeling anything but. "That was...incredible."

He looked up at me, his eyes meeting mine, and for a second, those eyes held the entire weight of the ocean.

"Thank you," he replied, a hint of surprise in his voice. He ran a hand through his long hair, pushing long, wet strands away from his face.

"I'm Sean," I said, extending a hand. "I've been watching you surf. You've got some serious talent."

He took my hand, his grip firm. "Cal Eaton. Calvin, really,

but I prefer Cal."

"Okay, Cal. Are you planning on riding those waves in the Big Wave Contest?" I asked.

His face darkened slightly, the joy of the waves replaced by a shadow of worry. "I'd love to, man. But I work most days, and I'm not sure if I can get so many days off."

"That's a shame," I replied genuinely. "You have something special. I know folks that...well, they're into the business side of surfing. Maybe I can talk to them about you and ask them to come down and watch you sometime? They're always on the lookout for new talent."

His eyes lit up, hope mingling with uncertainty. "Seriously? That would be...amazing. But look, I'm not sure. My old man doesn't support me in this. Thinks it's a waste of time and wants me to focus on my job and helping out at home. I don't want your friends coming down here and wasting their time."

I nodded, understanding more than he might have realized. "It's tough when your dreams clash with reality. How old are you?"

"I'll be twenty next month."

"Who taught and trained you to surf?"

"My uncle. My mother's brother. He was pretty good, but he never made it to the big time. My father swears that's what will happen to me. It won't. I know it won't, but nothing's going to change my old man's mind. So, I leave it alone."

"How about I call my friends, let them come down, observe you, and just see what happens? If it works out, you can go from there. If it doesn't, well, no sweat. How does that sound?"

"I dunno. My father won't like it."

"Sometimes, you've got to take a chance. Chase what sets your soul on fire. You're young, sure, but don't let these moments slip away."

We stood in silence for a while, two souls bound by the pull of the sea. "Tell you what," I finally said, "Let me make a few calls. No promises, but maybe, just maybe, we can find a way for you to chase that dream and still be there for your family."

I stood there for a moment, the ocean whispering its ancient tales around us, watching Cal look out at the ocean, his sanctuary. "If your friends want to come watch me, I'd like that, but it probably won't be in the contest. I love surfing more than anything, but it's not just about me. I've got responsibilities. I have to help my old man pay the bills and feed the family. I work at the lumber yard all day, every day. You can find me there when you know if anyone's coming."

I nodded, and Cal smiled, the weight on his shoulders seeming a little lighter. "Thanks, Mr. Sean. Thanks a lot. I...I've got to get to work now. I can't be late."

"No problem, and Just call me Sean. Not Mr. Hargrove," I said, sticking my hand out. He grasped it, and I gave him a firm shake. He grinned and turned away, striding confidently away. "Just keep riding those waves, Cal," I called after him. "The world deserves to see what you can do."

My mind was churning with possibilities as I headed for my house. So many people, trainers, managers, producers, and God knew who else would be interested in seeing Cal on the water, and unfortunately, not all of them would have his best interest in mind. I couldn't afford not to handle this with kid gloves. I didn't want to cause trouble between him and his father or give him any false hope, but he was the real thing, and I knew he could be more, do better, than work in a lumber yard.

CHAPTER SEVEN

I finished my meal of roasted chicken, potatoes, and vegetables and tossed my napkin on the table on top of a generous tip.

I nodded to Emmie that I was done, and strolled leisurely out of Lily's restaurant and stretched my arms over my head and to the side. I was full and tired, but not enough to go back to the house and crash. You'd think I'd feel stressed, but weirdly, it was the opposite. I felt really good. I was especially happy I'd found that gigantic bed frame and was able to get new mattresses and bedding. It was like sleeping on a cloud, and it was really all I needed. I could get myself a coffeemaker, but it was just easier to continue eating at Lily's.

I stepped off the sidewalk, intending to take the long way back along the beach front. The walk would settle my dinner, and I might be able to relax and watch something on the new television mounted over the fireplace. I hadn't gotten far when a familiar figure up ahead caught my attention. My pace slowed. No, it couldn't be. My heart did a little leap, half in shock, half in dread. That tall, lean stance, the way the shoulders were squared… it was unmistakably Drew. What the hell was he doing in Carmichael? He was supposed to be at the university. I'd been at Lizzie's' for the big send-off dinner, and I knew she'd put him on the train the next day. I felt a pull in my chest, a mix of curiosity and concern. He hadn't seen me yet, his back to me as he talked to two other young men, probably friends from school.

"Drew!" I called out, my voice laced with both surprise and irritation.

He turned, his wetsuit and hair still wet, glistening with droplets of seawater. "Uncle Sean! What are you doing here?"

We were stunned to see one another in the last place we'd ever expected to do so. Recovering from my shock and dismay, I stomped across the sand and approached Drew, my eyes narrowed and my tone stern. I was heedless of the two other young men standing behind him, fear dawning in their eyes.

"What am I doing here? What are you doing here, Drew? You're supposed to be at the University," I hissed. Lots of people, both residents and tourists, were out this evening, strolling along the boardwalk or heading toward the beach, likely planning to stroll there and watch the sunset. I did not want to make a bloody scene, but my anger was straining against a tight leash. His face fell, and he stared down at the sand.

"Yeah, well, about that, Uncle. I couldn't pass up this chance. I told the Academic Dean I needed to go home because my grandma was sick, and he said I could make up all of my work when I got back."

"No, you're going back tonight."

"No, I can't. I have to compete. I used everything I had to pay my fee. I can't go back to school." His face tightened; he stood straighter, taller, and looked me in the eye. He was only nineteen. He had no idea what he was doing by taking school so lightly. But eventually, I sighed, realizing he was at a crossroads, just like I had been at his age. "Drew, you can't skip classes. You're jeopardizing your future. Does Lizzie know you're here?"

He looked up at me, his eyes determined. "No. But you can understand that if things turn out like I believe they will, I'll turn pro, just like you and Uncle Josh did. Mom won't like it at first, but she'll understand it's in the blood."

I was taken aback by his words. "In the blood? Drew, surfing is a tough road. It's not all glamorous competitions and magazine covers. It's hard work and sacrifices. And I'd completed my second degree before I went pro."

He nodded, but his expression was resolute. "I know, but I need to get started. I'm already behind. You'd been surfing for five years by the time you were my age. I've only been surfing for two, and I didn't even join the Junior League. I've got to get started. I've got to get my name out there, and with the Big Wave competition coming up, I have a chance to prove myself and show everyone that I can make it. On my own."

I ran a hand down my face, from mouth to chin, feeling torn between my experiences and Drew's dreams, and wanting to make him understand, I spoke slowly. "Drew, this competition is no joke. It's dangerous, and those waves can be unpredictable. You have to think about your safety."

Drew's voice held a hint of frustration. "You don't understand. This is my shot, my opportunity to make a name for myself. I've been training hard and believe I can do it."

We stood there, the ocean's waves crashing in the background, and tension was thick between us. I understood he was enthralled with the allure of chasing his dreams, but I wanted him to understand the harsh realities of the surfing world.

"Drew," I finally said, ready to make him a deal. "I want you to pursue your passion, but not at the expense of your education and safety. Finish your degree, and then, if you still want to chase the pro surfer dream, I'll help do it with a plan and be your backup."

He looked at me with a mixture of dismay and determination. "I hear you, but I can't give up on this opportunity. I have to try."

He turned and tossed his board in the back of the truck and turned his buddies. "You ready to eat?" He asked them, and they nodded their assent. They were apparently frozen in their tracks, seeing me, and Drew grimaced at them before turning back to look at me.

"Is the Food at Lily's any good? I'm starving."

"Starving, are you? How long have you been here?"

"Two days. We finished up our hamper of sandwiches yesterday."

"Mmmph!" I grunted. "You got money?"

"Some."

"Where are you staying?"

"We'll, we haven't worked that out yet. We slept in the truck on the road."

"Shit, Drew." I couldn't believe him. None of this made any sense. "C'mon. I'll buy you guys some dinner, and then you come back to the house with me. The three of you."

"Okay, but what house? You're renting someplace out here?"

"No. As a matter of fact, take my card and tell Miss Lily, the lady at the front desk, that you're my nephews. Take this address. When you guys finish eating, come out to the house. I need to check on a few things before you get there.

I didn't bother watching them go inside Lily's. Instead, before driving back to the house, I picked up three inflatable mattresses and bedding. There were two empty bedrooms upstairs down the hall from mine that would be sufficient for three young men, each one close to, if not over, six feet tall.

Drew and his friends were blown away by the house and immediately dragged their things into the two empty bedrooms. They parked their truck next to mine at the turnaround at the end of the road, leaving the driveway free for the workers. I hadn't expected to share my digs with anyone, much less three exuberant young men, nor my early mornings on the water with them, but it became routine almost immediately.

I was a bit hesitant to surf with them. I felt like their nanny, trying to keep my eye on them and staying within range of reaching them should I need to. I was always on guard, not willing to let anything happen to any one of them, and that made me overwrought.

At night, I found myself tossing and turning in bed, unable to escape my fears. Each time I closed my eyes, vivid and distressing scenarios played out in my imagination. I would see Drew bobbing on his surfboard in the open ocean, foolishly facing monstrous waves that seemed intent on swallowing him whole. The turbulent waters would churn and roar, becoming an unforgiving force of nature, and he'd be overturned and struggle to keep his head above the surface. As the waves began to batter him, I'd watched in horror as he flailed about, as he fought from being dragged into the abyss. Though the horrors were only in my imagination, my heart pounded in my chest, and my breath caught in my throat. Unable to awaken, the scenarios would play out with me desperately scanning the tumultuous waters, searching for any sign of him. But there was only chaos. The ocean showed no mercy, and I would never reach him in time. Trying as hard as I might, I wouldn't be able to save him.

Another scenario would have Drew washing ashore, battered and bruised, his surfboard in pieces, the fear in his eyes mirroring my own. I would rush to his side, my voice choked with desperation. "Drew, are you okay?" But he couldn't respond. His body would be limp, his breathing shallow. Panic coursed through me as I tried to pick him up, fighting against the rushing tide that threatened to drag us both into the water.

With a gasp, I'd jolt awake, my heart racing and my pillow and bedding soaked in sweat. The room would be bathed in the pale light of dawn, and I'd hear the distant sound of the ocean, serving as a haunting reminder of my nightmare. I rarely went back to sleep after these dreams.

It was difficult to shake the overwhelming dread of Drew

in peril etched in my mind. I felt trapped and powerless to save him, and I know this profoundly impacted my initial struggle with the PTSD I knew I had, intensifying the guilt and anxiety that plagued me.

The solace I'd found here in Carmichael and the labor of fixing up the house had been shattered. Despite my efforts to move forward, my condition, which I believed had been mild, had dramatically escalated, forcing me to grapple with the complex and overwhelming emotions I'd hoped to escape when I embarked on my road trip.

I soon stopped surfing with the boys. I'd watch them instead from the shallows, where I'd sit on my board and watch Drew paddle into the open ocean, feeling both pride and dread. Pride in his determination to become better but dreading what could go wrong. Sometimes, I'd stay on the beach, sitting high up on the giant boulders scattered at the bottom of the bluff, and watch from a distance, or I'd paced back and forth on the sand, my eyes alert and constantly scanning for signs of the imminent danger and disaster my mind conjured. My eyes would track Drew's every move with a scrutinizing intensity that bordered on obsession. I told myself it was out of concern, out of a desire to keep him safe, but deep down, it was driven by the fear that disaster was lurking just beneath the surface. Fear had taken root in my soul, and even though I could see that Drew was a capable surfer, it shook my faith in his abilities. I became a silent sentinel, a guardian watching over him, ready to act at the slightest hint of trouble.

~

I returned home around mid-morning after watching some of the local boys surf and practically ran into Drew, who was pacing back and forth on the patio, talking on his mobile phone.

He looked distressed, and I immediately knew he was talking to his mother. I'd been meaning to talk to him again about surfing, his future, and going back to school, so I hung around thinking it might be a good time to try and talk some sense into him once he got off the phone. He plopped down on the new patio furniture next to me after hanging up.

"Good morning, Uncle. Have you been to breakfast?"

"No, I went down to the beach. Were you talking to Lizzie?" He looked up at me, his expression tight.

"Yeah. She wanted to know how my classes were going."

"You didn't tell her the truth, I take it."

His shoulders were hunched, and he shook his head. "No. And I feel bad for it."

"It's painful lying to our mothers. They only mean well for us."

"I know. But Mom will understand and hopefully forgive me when this is over. She'll see how much it means to me."

"You don't think she'll understand now? It's not like it's her first go-round. She's been through this before."

"Yeah, I know, but she was your sister, not your mother. She'll be mad as a hornet," he said, grinning up at me. "She'll look at me the way you do."

"Oh? And how do I look at you?" I asked with fake indignation.

"Like I'm the biggest blockhead for throwing away my education. You give me lectures about school and my future, and I get it, but she'll nag me to death."

I laughed, though it was no laughing matter. "Drew," I began, the weight of years bearing down on me, "I get it, the allure of going pro right away, the money, the fame. But trust me on this one: University first makes a ton of sense. And not everybody makes it."

Drew's jaw set, a clear indication he wasn't budging. "I've seen the contracts. The money's good. Why should I wait?"

I sighed. "Look at me. I'm thirty-six years old and a prime example of how quickly it can all come crashing down around you. I'm not saying this to scare you. I'm saying it because it's true, and I care about you and your future."

He looked away, a sign that he was wrestling with his thoughts. "I get where you're coming from, but this is my decision, and I think it's the right one for me. I can always go back for an education."

"Drew," I pressed, "all I'm asking is for you to think it over. Weigh the pros and cons. The game isn't going anywhere, just like you think school isn't going anywhere. But the opportunities you can get at the university? Those are once-in-a-lifetime."

"This is my shot. I need to take it." The firmness in his voice made my heart sink. I knew Drew was stubborn, much like I had been at his age. "I don't want you to make the same mistakes I did," I said softly, my voice almost breaking.

Drew's eyes met mine, and for a moment, I saw a hint of vulnerability. "I love you, Uncle Sean, and I appreciate your concern, truly, but I need to follow my gut, and I'm going for it."

I took a deep breath, my chest heavy with the weight of potential outcomes. The last thing I wanted was to alienate my nephew. "Just remember, whatever you decide, I'll always be here for you. But I had to voice my concerns, you know?"

Drew gave a small nod, a glint of appreciation in his eyes. "I know. I was hoping you'd be back soon. I've been wanting to ask you to train me and help me prepare for this competition. I'm facing some stiff competition from the locals. One guy, Cal something-or-other, is the one we all have to beat."

"I've seen him a few times. He's good."

"He's better than good, even I can see that, but I'm not afraid to go up against him."

"You could probably do with some training. Let me give some thought to how I can help you, okay? Then we'll talk."

"Awesome. I'm going to head out. We'll stop at Lily's for lunch. Maybe we'll see you there."

" Yeah, okay."

As he clamored back up the stairs and went inside to get his surfboard, I knew we'd passed some threshold. I knew he was bound and determined to follow this path. I had to reconcile myself to letting him make his own decisions, even if they broke my heart. I pulled out my phone and dialed Josh's mobile number. He answered on the first ring.

"What are you doing?" I asked, without preamble.

"Having coffee on the front porch. The sunrise was spectacular this morning."

I chuckled. "Front porch? Where are you?"

"The Crags. I drove up a couple of days ago to hang out with Charlie."

"Really? How long are you staying?"

" I dunno. What's going on?"

"It's a long story. I'm not far from there. I'm in Carmichael."

"What's happening in Carmichael? Where is Carmichael? I thought you were in Sydney with your family. Is everything alright?"

"Yes, and no. I can drive up this afternoon. I'm glad you're with Charlie. I kinda want to talk to you both."

"Okay."

"You doing okay? Sleeping alright?"

"Yeah, sometimes."

I exhaled slowly, softly. I knew what that meant. Josh's night terrors were debilitating, keeping him awake for days and nights at a time. I could plainly recall him sitting up all night at the beach house in San Diego, staring out at the ocean, a glass of whiskey in his hand. The silence lengthened. We were staring at the same ocean but from different geographical points.

"I'll be up this afternoon."

"Yeah, okay. I'll tell Charlie. Bring some treats and packs of coffee. He's like a kid at Christmas when we come bearing gifts."

"Anything in particular?"

"Just the coffee. Fine ground. The good stuff. Anything else is fine. Charlie loves surprises."

"How's he doing?"

"He still gets around. Just a little slower. Still nags."

"That's good. I'll see you guys soon."

I hung up and put my phone in my pocket as I stood up. I felt better for deciding to talk to Josh and Charlie. They would help me untie all the knots I'd worked myself into and help me get over myself. I could make a few phone calls and pull in a few favors to have someone come out to see Cal. I'm sure he has what it took to shine on the surf circuit, but as unlikely as it might seem, Cal might not want that. I might be stepping out on a limb.

Drew, however, was another bucket of fish. He was practically salivating over getting on the circuit and receiving sponsorships and all the notoriety. I had to help him over the next few weeks. Just until this competition is over, or I could destroy any future I may have with him and damage the one I had with my sister, Elizabeth. Helping him train for this competition might be the best thing I could do for him.

CHAPTER
EIGHT

I threw some clothes in my small duffle bag and called Drew to let him know my plans.

Lara hadn't arrived at the house before I was ready to leave, attending to an emergency on another site, but her crew was there doing some finishing work. I let them know I had some business to attend to and reminded them my nephew and his friends were staying in the house. However, I also sent her a text. I drove to Lily's and put in a huge order for baked goods, including bread, cakes and pies, and a half-dozen or so dinners packed to go. I also set up a tab on my credit card for the boys to eat. I then shopped for coffee and biscuits, deli meats and various cheeses, fruits of every kind, condiments, beer and pale ale; everything I thought Charlie might like. If he was like a kid at Christmas, then I was not about to disappoint. The tally was huge, but I grinned as I packed it all in the back of the truck and locked it down with the tonneau cover.

As I'd told Josh, I was only a couple of hours from them, and the traffic was good all the suway there. I turned off at the exit for Yakon and followed the road that was little more than a rut cut through the underbrush that led to the Crags. The entire way up, I gagged on the earthy aroma of the wet, rotting coastal vegetation, mingling with the fishy small and saltwater in the air.

The smell was unimaginably foul, but at least nothing squelched beneath my tires. I continued up the road until it turned into a stony trail, and the Crags finally came into view, a magnificent, weathered wooden structure standing as a testament to the passage of time.

The house, named for the type of cliff on which it was built and blended into almost perfectly, was a solid structure of ancient timber and brown and gray stone. The jutting, granite precipice on which the building stood overlooked the vast, churning expanse of the sea and had withstood the ocean's encroaching waves and salty mists for eons. When Josh bought the place, he'd modernized the inside, adding conveniences for Charlie, who was old even then but left the exterior as it was.

I pulled the truck around next to Josh's sleek, German-manufactured car and carried all the bags inside. After greeting Charlie and grabbing a beer, I joined Josh on the front porch. The wooden planks beneath my feet creaked and groaned as I rocked back and forth in the old porch chair and looked out towards the horizon, a blurred line where the ocean's dark blue met the cerulean blue of the late afternoon sky. We were perched on the edge of the world. Or so it felt.

Though it was mid-summer and steamy hot in the lower climes, the air up here was cool enough for a thin jacket or jumper, something against the stiff wind howling up from the water below. Locks of my hair whipped around, and I could taste the salt on my lips.

"Man," I mumbled, squinting against the wind. "Whoever

built this place picked one helluva spot, didn't they?"

Josh chuckled, "It is something, isn't it? It has to be the best view in the world."

Far below, tiny figures moved on the waves. Surfers. They looked like small specks from up here, brave souls dancing with the tumultuous sea. The sea was a powerful, unpredictable entity, and the thought of what lay beneath its surface sent shivers down my spine. No doubt there were sharks down there, lurking in the depths. And pods of dolphins, known to playfully bump surfers off their boards. And majestic, migrating whales whose sheer size was a danger in and of itself. I let out a sigh, the weight of my thoughts evident. Josh looked over, his usually cheerful eyes filled with concern.

"You okay, man?"

I hesitated, "I dunno. Drew skipped classes and turned up in Carmichael to enter the Big Wave Competition. He has technique, but he's not an inspired surfer like Cal Easton. Cal could be a champion surfer. He's that good, and he's not even twenty yet. I recorded him on my phone. I wanted you to see him." I tapped through my photo gallery until I found the video and handed him my phone. "Here," I began, my voice pitched with excitement. "Watch this."

I watched him as he watched the three-minute video. The screen showed Cal paddling hard against the waves, his every muscle defined and poised for action. Suddenly, a monstrous wave formed behind him, and with a swift turn, he caught it just as it began to break. The camera shook slightly, probably due to my uncontrollable excitement while filming. He moved as if the board was an extension of himself. He swerved left, then cut right, the wave curling beautifully around him as he shot through its barrel. Water cascaded around him, shimmering like a million diamonds in the sun, but Cal emerged from the other side, triumphant and electrified.

Josh nodded slowly, understanding. "He is good, Sean. One of the best I've seen in a long while."

"I know, right. I've talked to him. He works seven days in a lumber yard, from open to close, for not much more than minimum wage. He said I could talk to some people and invite them down to observe him surf, but now Drew's shown up wanting the same thing. I wanted Drew and his friends to turn right around and go back to the university. Is it right for me to encourage Cal to go pro? They're about the same age, with the same dream… is it right for one and not the other? And the ocean… it's not just waves and surfboards. There's a whole world beneath. What if something happens, especially on my watch? Lizzie will never forgive me. I couldn't forgive myself. It's been difficult enough with you and Colin…."

"Did you record Drew?"

"I did." I scrolled through more pictures and found the video of Drew. Josh leaned back, rocking his straight-back chair onto its back legs, and watched the video of Drew. I knew he saw Drew had good technique, skill and some talent, but he wasn't inspired or inspiring. That was something a trainer couldn't instill in an athlete. He had to have that special quality, or he didn't. Drew didn't, but rigor, skill and technique could take him far. I stared out at the horizon. I knew I shouldn't be comparing them. Doing so was like comparing apples and oranges. Cal had learned to surf as a young child. Drew only had a few years of experience.

Josh gave me back my phone, took a sip from his glass and cleared his throat. I waited, knowing he was trying to find the right words.

"We can't live our lives on *what-ifs*, Sean. If we did, we'd never do anything. But I get it. He's your nephew, your sister's son. You worry."

I took another sip of my beer, the cold liquid doing little to quench the heat of my worry. "I do. The sea is vast, wild, and untamed. We're just tiny specks in comparison."

Josh was quiet for a moment, letting the wind carry our words away. I blew out a tense breath.

"You ever worry about all the creatures beneath the surface?" I asked, my voice barely above a whisper.

"All the time," he admitted. "We never know what's lurking below."

A tense silence settled between us, broken only by the distant shouts of the surfers and the relentless crash of waves against the bluff.

"Have you been back on the water since you've been back?" I pressed.

He shook his head, a frown appearing momentarily on his face. "I can't."

"No, it's still too soon," I said, remembering how he had frozen up, standing hip-deep in the ocean, and how he had puked his guts out after forcing himself to paddle out for Colin's memorial. There was a chance he would never go back into the water again, but then some people lived their whole lives without ever getting on a surfboard or taking a swim in the ocean.

Josh took a deep breath before turning to me. "The ocean is like life for some people, you know? There's beauty, danger, and uncertainty. But when I used to ride a wave, even for just a moment, all that faded away, and it was just me and the water, and in that moment, I used to feel alive. Now, all I feel is abject terror. I don't want to go back in. Not ever."

I stared at him, struck by the simplicity of his words. He was right. Life was uncertain and full of risks and challenges. But there were also moments of pure, unbridled joy. I continued to surf even weeks after the Shark attack. I'd even gone back in immediately to help coast guard search-and-rescuers search for Colin, to bring his body out if we found it. I wasn't afraid for myself. Drew made me afraid. I was terrified that something might happen to him.

"I know I'm not one to offer sage advice, but you have to let it all go, Sean. What's the saying? *Let go and let God?* Yeah, you gotta let go. You cannot control anyone's destiny, and you cannot let your fears control you."

"Yeah, you're right," I murmured, not sure I could just let go.

He clinked his glass of fresh juice against my beer bottle. "Anytime, buddy."

We sat silently, watching the surfers below, each lost in our thoughts. Then Josh began laughing, a carefree belly laugh I hadn't heard in a long time.

"You know something," he began, his gaze drifting toward the horizon, "I think you and Drew are like... two peas in a pod. He reminds me of you at his age."

I raised an eyebrow, my curiosity piqued. "What do you mean?"

Josh let out another big chuckle. "Well, for one, it seems he's got that same determination and bullheadedness you have. You would not let me or Colin beat you out there on those waves, and if we did, we damn well earned it."

I couldn't help but grin at the comparison. Of all people, he knew how stubborn I could be and have always been when it came to being the best.

"That sounds more like you, my friend. You were the one with the drive, a natural on the water. I'm a logical person, and I approached it by perfecting my technique. I could understand it from that perspective, but you... it just flowed for you."

"You both have the drive to push yourselves beyond your limits. Some things came easy for me, other things…not so much, but you…you worked your ass off for everything. It's what made you a legend in the surfing world, Sean. Maybe it'll happen for him the same way."

I nodded in understanding. "I get it, man. I hope you're right.

Josh placed a hand on my chair, offering reassurance. "It's a tough balance between supporting his passion and keeping him safe. But remember, you turned out just fine."

Sean smiled gratefully at Josh's words. "If being a jittery old man is alright, I want better for him. We, at least, finished at the University. He's so impatient, he wants it all right now."

"They call it youth. Wisdom comes with age," Charlie said as he opened the screen door and looked around at us. "Lunch is ready. Sean brought us hot food, fresh fruit, and cold beer. Looks like he brought us some sweets, too. Come on in and eat. And, who's a jittery old man?" he asked, pushing the screen door open again.

"Not me," Josh replied. "I have nerves of steel."

I stayed the night at the Crags, enjoying the batter between Charlie, Josh and myself and reviewing the details of all of the videos I'd taken of both Cal and Drew on the water. Josh was animated, critiquing their performances, and I had to admit he was spot on. Especially the one of Drew. His performance was decent, but in contrast to Cal's earlier feat, it paled. He wobbled a few times and missed a couple of turns, even though he man-aged to ride his waves to their end. He was decent, no doubt, but Cal... Cal was just extraordinary.

Josh let out a whistle. "Damn! That was... That was insane!" He yelled across the room to me. "Cal has some serious skills."

I grinned, unable to hide my pride. "I know, right! It was like watching art in motion. Every turn, every move, just perfect."

Josh leaned toward me and pointed the phone at the massive television mounted on the wall, having cast the videos I'd re-corded there. I looked to where he was pointing, seeing the part where Cal shot through the barrel on the replay. "Look at that precision," he said, freezing the shot. "And the balance! It's like he was born for this."

"He probably was," I replied thoughtfully. "When we were kids, we had this connection with the water. He has it, too. It's like he's in sync with the waves."

Josh nodded, his eyes still glued to the screen. "And Drew?"

I shrugged, "He's good. Could be better than most, but Cal's on another level."

Josh looked up, his eyes serious. "You need to show this to some sponsors or something. This is pro-level stuff. Cal has what it takes."

A warmth spread through my chest. "Thanks, man. I needed to hear that. Sometimes, it's hard to trust my own judgment, but this," I gestured to the video, "this is undeniable."

Josh got up, strode over to me, and clapped me on the back. "It is. And you know what? You're a damn good uncle for supporting Drew and a mentor for helping Cal. They're lucky to have you."

I smiled, taking another sip of my beer. "And I'm lucky to have them around. You, Charlie…them, you're all my family. I've been blessed, and I want to give back. Help another generation, make it a little easier for surfers like Cal to get the breaks."

I went to bed that night, the weight of my earlier worries replaced by a renewed sense of hope and excitement. As the stars began to emerge, one by one, in the night sky, I couldn't help but think that, just like those stars, some people were meant to shine brighter than others. And Cal? I believed Cal was one of them.

CHAPTER NINE

The drive back to Carmichael was quick and without incident, but it was nearly sunset when I pulled up in front of the house.

I noticed that the boys' truck was gone, but Lara's car was parked out front. I pulled up behind it, hopped out, and headed for the front stairs. She stepped out on the porch, and I sucked in my breath. I've seen her in work clothes every day I've known her, her hair pulled back into a neat ponytail, and sometimes with oversized glasses on. But today, seeing her smiling at me bowled me over. God, she was stunning. I froze at the bottom of the steps, just taking her in, the world narrowing down to this single moment. Maybe it was the unexpectedness of it all, or maybe it was just her, but words seemed to fail me. I felt like someone had let all of the air out of me.

"Sean! You're home," she blurted out, while at the same time, I stammered, "Lara, what a... surprise. I was just coming back from..."

We'd both begun to speak at once, tripping over our words, and we stopped at the same time, an awkward silence stretching between us. I cleared my throat, trying to recover some semblance of composure.

"Sorry," I said. "You go first."

Her cheeks tinted with a hint of pink, but her excitement

couldn't be contained. "Most of the stuff we've been waiting on should be here by the end of the week. I just got the confirmation, and I wanted to tell you in person."

My heart rate quickened, both from her news and from her proximity. "That's... that's great news, Lara." A sheepish grin tugged at my lips. For a moment, we stood there, the tension of the unexpected encounter palpable. "Thanks for the update," I managed, my voice slightly unsteady. "I... I appreciate it. And you. Being here, I mean."

She smiled that radiant, captivating smile, and suddenly, the world felt a little brighter. "No problem. I also came to check the layout again. I didn't want to hold everybody up because I changed my mind."

"Of course. I understand." My heart was thudding loudly in my chest, and I wanted to say something witty or charming, but words escaped me. I could only stand there, taking in the sight of her. Every interaction with her was like stepping back into the maelstrom of high school emotions. That cocktail of nerves, excitement, and dread. It was both exhilarating and maddeningly frustrating. It wasn't just the way she looked or the way she spoke but rather the whirlwind of feelings she stirred within me.

Here I stood, reduced to the emotional state of a teenager around her. It was maddening. Women—heiresses, movie stars and models, debutantes and wealthy widows, have all fallen to my celebrity and my charms even before I'd gained my majority. Championship surfers were a hot commodity on the National and International circuits, yet here I was, rendered utterly self-conscious by the sight of this woman, with echoes of locker-lined hallways and adolescent uncertainties swirling around inside me. I knew I sometimes over-analyzed even the simplest interactions with her. An offhand comment she made while working together, the tilt of her head, that half-smile she sometimes wore. And each one became a puzzle that made me wonder if she felt something for me, something unprofessional. Or was I just misreading signs like a teen with his first crush?

Thus far, I'd been able to shake off these feelings, but every time I saw her, I felt like I was teetering on the edge of boyish infatuation and the mature restraint of adulthood. This turmoil, this teenage angst, was a thrilling reminder of youth but also a disconcerting jumble of emotions. It made me vulnerable around her and kept me on my toes. Most unsettlingly, however, it left me wanting something more.

"I saw your note about your nephew and his friends and I yesterday met them on their way to the ocean. They were perfect gentlemen. They said they'd come down to compete in the Big Wave competition." She opened the screen door wider and moved aside to let me in the house. I tramped up the stairs and followed her inside.

"Yeah, it's good to know they exercised good manners, even if they didn't show good sense."

"How so?"

"Long story," I said as I set my duffle bag down and looked around. The interior looked as good as the exterior. The remaining kitchen fixtures and comfortable furnishings were going to really set it out.

"So, the crews are done for the day?" I asked, turning to look at her again."

"Just finishing up. I'm getting ready to check on another job on the south end of town. Smaller, just a kitchen refresh. But I'm glad to run into you."

"Same."

"Marie, my interior designer, and her team will need access to the house and no peeking until they're done. Is that okay with you?"

"Absolutely."

"Good. We'll set the date when everything comes in. I've got to run, but I'll see you tomorrow."

I smiled, nodded, and watched her walk out the front door. Shaking my head, I picked up my bag and carried it upstairs to my room.

I don't know when the boys got home that night, but the next morning, I awakened them right after dawn, which was much earlier than they're used to getting up, and we took the stairs down the rock face. Standing on the sand, I have them move around so that they are facing me so that I can see their faces. They're dressed in board shorts and long-sleeved rash guards, their surfboards tucked under their arms like shields of war. They're also wide awake, their faces a mix of excitement and apprehension, probably mirroring my own.

"Good morning," I greet, forcing a smile to mask the weight of what I'm about to tell them.

"What's up, Uncle?" Drew asks, his voice tinged with curiosity. "You've been MIA for a couple of days."

"Yeah? It's only been two days, Drew. I had to go up to see Josh and Charlie. But I'm back now," I said, choosing my words carefully.

"So, what's the plan? We're only a few weeks away from the competition," Art chimes in, ever the planner.

I took a deep breath, looked each of them in the eye, and spilled it. "Look, if we're going to do this, we have to do it right. I'm going to help you guys, and it's going to be tough. But if you stick with it, you'll not just survive those waves; you'll own them. It's all about balance and instinct." Drew was watching me so intently I felt the weight of responsibility on my shoulders. For him, it wasn't just about teaching him to surf; it was about passing on a legacy. His eyes were eager, searching mine for guidance.

"How did you do it?" Arthur asked. Drew had probably shared stories with them about me, but I'd never taken the time to talk to them myself. I hadn't taken much time with Drew either since he'd shown up here, not beyond the lectures I'd given him. A deep sigh escaped me.

"It wasn't just about getting on a board and letting the waves take me," I answered. "It was about understanding the rhythm, feeling the ocean, and knowing when to let go." The nerves in my stomach tighten.

"That's what I want from you. Take deep breaths and feel the water beneath you. It's alive, moving, shifting. Respect it, and it will respect you."

Drew and Will nodded, the weight of my words sinking in. I remember the countless times I was pulled under, the moments of panic, the need to surface, to breathe. But I also remember the exhilaration, the freedom.

"I won't lie. It's going to be tough," I confess. "There will be moments when you'll want to give up, when the ocean will test you, but remember, every wave you conquer, every challenge you overcome, will shape you into the surfer you're meant to be." I feel a pang of nostalgia. The early mornings, the sore muscles, the taste of salt on my lips.

"When I started, I was lost. The ocean was my teacher, my mentor. It showed me my strengths and exposed my weaknesses. But that's why I'm here, so you won't be so lost. I'm here to help you."

A determined glint shines in Drew's eyes. "I'm ready."

My heart swelled with pride. "We're going to work on drills for a couple of days. I need to see the basics—like your balance and footwork, your timing, turns, and duck dives. If and when I'm satisfied that you know what you're doing out there, we'll move on to cut-backs, transitions, and maybe some aerials. We'll work on smoothing out your tubing, too. We don't have a lot of time, so you're going to have to come out twice a day and practice the things I'm teaching you. I'll come out with you in the mornings, we'll go through drills, and then you'll come back out during the day and evenings to practice on your own. You ready for this?"

"When do we start?" Will asked, a determined gleam in his eyes.

"Right now. So, line up! We're going to paddle out together." I announce, walking past them and wading into the surf. The water is cool against my skin, and they follow me in, setting their boards on the water's edge and squaring their shoulders as if preparing for battle.

"I want you to paddle with strong strokes, efficiency, and rhythm. If you're out of sync, you're gonna tire yourself out before even catching a wave. Now, on my mark... Go!"

I assessed each of them as they pushed off into the water, their arms slicing through the ocean's surface. I can see their muscles strain with each stroke, and it dawns on me how much is riding on this training. Drew's arms flail a bit; he's putting in the effort, but he's wasting energy. Art's got a good tempo going but needs to dig deeper with his hands. And Will... well, Will is struggling to find a rhythm, his arms and legs out of sync as if he's fighting the ocean instead of becoming one with it. I think they're trying too hard, trying to impress me.

"Push!" I yell, urging them on as I paddle out behind them. I see Drew glance over at Art, the competitive spirit in his eyes igniting. That's what I want—them pushing each other to be better.

I have them turn around at the buoy, the halfway point, and paddle back to me. They're gasping for air but giving it their all. I have them straddle their boards and look at me.

"In a competition like the one you've entered, you can't start out like it's a relaxing morning on the water. It's a race against every person on the water with you." They nod, eyes locked onto mine. "Tonight, you work on getting to the line faster. Now. I want to see you take a wave. I want you to read the ocean like it's your opponent. Get it wrong, and you'll wipe out before you even start. I'll go first, then you, Drew, Art, then you, Will. I want to see what you've got."

I lead the way, paddling out past the break, and the boys follow suit. I position myself where the sets are rolling in, waiting for the perfect teaching moment. The ocean swells beneath us, its rhythmic breathing setting the tone for the lesson. I point at it as it rolls towards me. Timing it perfectly, I paddle hard and pop up, riding the wave smoothly before it breaks. It's a short ride but enough to demonstrate the skill involved. I know they're not at my level, but I want them to see and try to imitate what I do."

"Alright, your turn," I say, paddling back to where they're bobbing like buoys. "It's all about timing and commitment. Hesitate, and the wave will own you."

Drew is up first. His eyes narrow as he spots a wave forming in the distance and starts paddling but mistimes it, taking off too early. The wave crashes over him, and he wipes out, reemerging with a mouthful of saltwater and a bruised ego.

Art takes the cue, his eyes locked onto an approaching wave. He waits, paddles at the right moment, and pops up just as the wave begins to curl. He rides it all the way in, whooping in exhilaration as he does. I nod approvingly. Will follows. His paddling is a little shaky but committed. He catches the wave but loses balance halfway, tumbling into the foam. Not perfect, but better. As they paddle back to regroup, I can't help but feel a mix of pride and concern. They're learning, but time is running out. Still, watching Art nail that wave gives me hope.

"What did you do wrong?" I asked them, and Drew spoke up first.

"I went for it too early." I nodded, glad he understood.

"My timing was off, and it threw everything off."

"Right. What about you, Art? Anything you can improve?"

"Confidence. I was really nervous, but I believed I could do it."

"Absolutely. And You need to practice doing it as much as you can, tonight and every night. You don't want the judges deducting points right off the bat. You'll never make those points up. I want you to do it one more time, then we'll work on your transitions."

I'm proud of them and their will to succeed and willingness to take cues from me. I won't hold them back to make sure they're executing perfectly. They don't have time for that, but I do want them to have a good showing, and as long as they practice as much as they have time, they should make it past the elimination heats.

We'd been out for a few hours, and the sun was pretty high in the sky, warming the water and our skin. My stomach protested loudly, and I knew the boys were starving. They're always starving. I'm sure they're still serving breakfast at the diner, and I wave them in. Probably not a moment too soon. Art looks like he's all in, and I'm sure that's Will's stomach grumbling that I hear.

"Get dressed, and I'll meet you down at the diner." They leap and whoop cheerfully and take off across the sand. I follow a little more leisurely, giving them time to clear out of the shared bathroom.

We were out most of the day. The boys were like sponges, soaking up everything I could give them. After lunch, we did some mental conditioning to help them with their nerves as well as their overabundance of energy, a result of their nerves. I brought in some elements of visualization and breath control techniques to help them stay focused and calm under pressure. After dinner, they chilled out for a while and then went back out to practice. I remained at the house, chilling with the remote in my hand.

We followed our routine the rest of the week, and as promised, I moved them on to the next group of skills—cut back and re-entry maneuvers, faster and tighter carving, and floating, which is essentially riding over the whitewater on a breaking wave. At night, they go through all of the drills, from the first through the last. If, after a couple of days, they look good, I'd put them through the next set.

We've only got another ten days to Opening Day, and this morning, I'm in a good mood. The waves are firing, like Mother Nature's cranked up the volume, and they're just begging to be shredded. I looked at the boys, hoping I was making the right decision. If they were as determined to surf the Challenge against more experienced surfers as they seemed to be, I had to know what they had, and these five or six-footers would give them a good workout.

"Alright, you guys, we're going aerial," I announce, my eyes meeting theirs. A mixture of excitement and uncertainty ripples through them. In the time I'd been working with them, I'd never let them perform tricks. But aerials are a staple of competitive surfing, and nailing them shows you've got mastery over your board and the wave.

"Listen up," I continue, "Go out there and have fun. I want to see your best tricks. I want to see you defy gravity. You ready to show me what you can do?" They whoop like schoolboys, jumping and high-fiving each other like I've given them an extra period of recess.

I run out into the waves and paddle out. They follow at a distance, their excitement electric in the air. I spot a promising set rolling in and motion for them to watch me. I paddle hard, feeling the wave lift me, and then I pop up. Approaching the lip, I crouch low and then spring upwards, launching myself and my board into the air. For a split second, I'm flying. I landed smoothly and rode out the wave. As I paddle back to them. Their awe is palpable, and from their expressions, I can tell they're itching to show off. Drew goes first. He paddles into a wave and pops up, but then, he hesitates at the critical moment. I can't tell what's happening except that Drew bails and crashes into the foam below. I watch as he resurfaces and gets back on board to go for another run. I blow out a breath and settle back on my own board.

Art is up next. His takeoff is clean, and as he approaches the lip, he springs up, gaining air. For a second, it looks like he's going to nail it, but then he loses control, his board flipping away from him as he spills into the water.

"Close, Art. You're almost there. Keep that board under control," I shout encouragingly.

Finally, it's Will's turn. He's been the underdog in all this, but I see a spark in his eyes. He paddles into the wave, pops up, and as he reaches the lip, he goes for it. He leaps, tucking his knees, and for a heartbeat, he soars—before landing back on his board and riding the wave out.

"Dammit, Will! That's what I'm talking about!" I can't help but hoot as he rides back, his face flushed with triumph.

"Alright, we're running it again. Drew, Art—you've seen what you're up against. Go for it," I yell.

As they position themselves on the line, I can't shake off the weight of what we're doing here. We're not playing out here, though it is fun. This is transformation. From riders to flyers, from followers to leaders. And as their coach and their mentor, I feel a sense of responsibility heavier than all the water in the ocean. What we're doing is not just about the waves, the tricks, or even the looming competition. It's about pushing limits and breaking barriers—both in the ocean and in ourselves.

They set themselves up for the next set of waves, and I hope they realize this is more than just a drill. This is a lesson in life. To go aerial, to fly, you have to commit. You have to take the leap, knowing you might crash and burn. But if you nail it, the feeling is like no other. It's freedom, it's exhilaration—it's pure, unadulterated pleasure, and right now, that's a lesson worth teaching.

The boys and I drove down to Lily's for dinner, getting back home a little later than usual. Pulling up to the house, I noticed the entire house was lit up, warm light shimmering through the new double-hung windows framed by dark drapery. I'd received a text from Lara with five numbers, 1-2-3-4-5, but no message. I parked the truck onto the empty driveway, and we all climbed out, slamming my doors with unnecessary force. I was first up the stairs and immediately saw the electronic lock on the door. I tapped in the five numbers in Lara's text, and the front door clicked open. I gave it a light push, and it swung open smoothly and quietly on new, oiled hinges. I was dumbfounded by what I saw, and the boys behind me were just as much in disbelief. This couldn't be the same place. It was as if we'd walked into a house from an upscale design magazine. The first thing I noticed was the scent—a blend of freshly cut wood, citrus, and leather, a fresh, hardy scent. I was glad Lara had gone with that because florals, Orientals, and potpourri were anathema to me.

What was once a cramped and dark living room was now light, airy, and expansive, a result of the new, extra-large windows they'd put in. The walls were painted in a soft gray, giving the space a modern feel. An oversized leather sofa and an incredible steel and glass coffee table faced the oversized, wall-mounted TV above the fireplace, anchored by a thick textured rug. The entire room was perfect. Perfect for Sunday afternoons and evenings watching soccer and football or just lounging around. I could hear Drew whistle as he came in behind me.

"Wow, Uncle Sean, this is like... wow!"

In the dining area, which blended seamlessly with the living room, stood an eight-foot table made of some oil-rubbed wood on a black steel base. Very chic, retro-looking leather chairs surrounded it, and elegant pendant lights hung above it. I rubbed my hand across the top of the chair back, enchanted with the fine, butter-soft texture.

The kitchen was open to the two main rooms, the sleek, modern cabinets contrasting beautifully with the black marble island and counter tops. Recessed lighting illuminated the workspace, and pendant lights hung above the island, their light sparkling and reflecting off the stainless-steel appliances. Five backless stools matching the dining chairs surrounded the massive island, making it the perfect space for morning coffee and quick meals and snacks. Arthur ran his hand over the smooth counter top, clearly impressed.

"This is some next-level stuff."

Will chimed in, "I could live here forever!"

I laughed, agreeing with him. "Ms. Finnegan's done an incredible job."

Drew came over and nudged me playfully. "Guess we should have a big party to celebrate, huh?"

I grinned, looking around the transformed space. "Absolutely. This is exactly how I imagined it. This is going to be a great vacation house."

A knock at the door brought our attention back to the living room, and Will opened the door. Lara stood on the porch with a vase of cut wildflowers in her arms.

"Lara, I said, surprised, and rushed to take her burden."

"You beat me back." She said, following me into the kitchen. I put the vase on the island, and she picked it up, taking it to the sink to fill it with water.

"Lucky for me, I had the code."

"I thought that was a nice touch. I assumed you'd figure it out quickly enough."

"I'm rather good at solving puzzles. I want to thank you. The whole place looks amazing."

"Did you go upstairs?"

"No. I wasn't expecting you to touch the upstairs."

"You can't have guests sleeping on inflatable mattresses for-ever. The bedrooms are set up, beds made, and bathrooms fully stocked. Oh, and I took the liberty of ordering some groceries for the pantry." She opened a panel in the wall, revealing a door and a sizeable room stocked with groceries. The house is com-pletely finished and ready for you to be your own guest."

"Thank you," I said, truly humbled.

"Actually, I have to give Marie's team a lot of the credit. I love the work they do, so I use them as often as I can."

"Thank you again, and give them my thanks as well."

"Is it worth the small fortune you shelled out?"

"Yes, that and more."

"Good. The last draft will come out of the account tomorrow."

"No problem."

Lara placed the flowers in the center of the island top and took a seat. I sat down beside her and turned so I could see her. I hadn't noticed until that moment that she was wearing her hair in loose curls that spilled over her shoulders, and she wasn't wearing overalls.

"You look very nice," I say inanely, wanting to take a closer sniff of the perfume she was wearing.

"Thank you." She blushed, which was also something new, and self-consciously picked up a curl and began twirling it around her finger. Her eyes, usually so focused and confident, now flitted around the room as if searching for something to land on. Clearing my throat, I leaned a bit closer and rubbed my palms against my jeans.

"Lara," I started, my voice quivering ever so slightly, betraying my emotions. She met my gaze, her soft blue eyes reflecting a myriad of emotions.

"Yes?"

This is it, Sean, old Boy, I thought. It's now or never. And I cleared my throat once more. "I've been thinking. Maybe we could... you know, celebrate the end of our project. With dinner. Somewhere nice, perhaps?" I quickly added. For a moment, she seemed taken aback. Her eyes widened slightly, and her fingers paused mid-twirl. I could feel each second stretching out, making the anticipation almost unbearable.

"Well, there's a quaint French restaurant in Mercy, which is a short drive from here. It'll be my treat," she said, grinning impishly. "In gratitude for that big check you just wrote."

"French, huh? Authentic French cuisine?"

"Yes. I've been a couple of times, and it's fantastic. I love their Duck a la Orange, but the ambiance is also lovely."

"Okay," I said, grinning back at her.

"I know it's a little drive over, but it's also a little escape from the local gossip, if you know what I mean. If we had a nice dinner here in town, the whole town would have us engaged by morning. Nothing gets by people around here." A deep pink blush suffused her cheeks, and her lips curved into that playful, infectious smile that I liked so much.

"Let's not fuel the fire, then. And I love French food. It's a date. then?" I confirmed.

She nodded, her smile brightening the room. "It's a date."

CHAPTER
TEN

The next morning, we were back in the water, and I decided to push the boys a lot harder today.

"The last one to the buoy and back has to cook dinner tonight! No takeout from Lily's tonight." I challenged them to get their muscles and blood warmed up. Instead of laughing and teasing one another like usual, they are silent and deadly serious as they race toward the buoy, their muscles burning. It's a close call, but Drew edges them out, a look of sheer determination on his face. It's funny to see them that determined, especially since I don't think either of them knew how to cook, and I wasn't trusting my stomach to the test.

"Alright, lads, it's time to dance," I say, grinning at them while leading them into the surf. "I'm talking about your rail-to-rail transitions. I want them smooth, controlled, and fluid."

They look at me, their expressions a mix of anticipation and curiosity. They've been getting much better at incorporating the things that I've been teaching them, but rail-to-rail was a step toward finesse, toward making their boards an extension of themselves. And to onlookers, they looked like they were dancing on the board. They would also get good points from the judges in deploying that skill.

"This is about quick and controlled shifts from one side of

the board to the other. It's a vital skill for sharp turns and for handling more complex waves," I explain, paddling fast to the line and getting into position. I scan the horizon for the right wave to demonstrate, and as I spot an incoming set, I shout over my shoulder. "Watch closely."

I feel the wave lift me up, and I pop to my feet. The board accelerates down the line. Now comes the dance: shifting my weight onto the right rail, I carve a smooth arc into the face of the wave. Then, with a seamless transition, I lean into the left rail, pulling off another arc, this one in the opposite direction.

As I ride out the wave and paddle back, I'm met with a trio of eager faces. "Your turn. Remember, it's about finesse, not force."

As usual, Drew is up first. His paddle is strong, his takeoff smooth. He tries shifting his weight, but it's too abrupt, and his board skips out from under him. A wipeout but a worthy attempt.

"Easy on the transition, Drew. Smooth, like you're swaying to some slow jam," I offer, suppressing a chuckle. Art takes the next wave, and I can see he's been paying attention. His movements are more graceful, and his transitions are nearly textbook. He rides out the wave, a broad grin splitting his face as he paddles back.

"Textbook, Art. Keep that up."

Will followed his attempt, not as fluid as Art but not as jerky as Drew. It's not perfect, but it's progress.

"You're getting there, Will. Keep practicing," I encourage as we paddle back out to do it all over again.

Each time they ride, I see them getting better, their boards becoming more in tune with their bodies and their surfboards. But I'm not just watching their technique; I'm watching them evolve, seeing their confidence build with each wave they dance on.

"You guys are getting it. But remember, it's not just about the moves. It's about making those transitions seamless, making your ride one fluid motion."

I watch them do it a few more times, and then I decide to change things up…again.

"Alright, so the last thing we're going to work on this morning is less about muscle and more about the mind," I announce as we sit on our boards in a circle, the noses of our boards touching as we bob gently on the water's surface. Blank faces stare back at me. They're still high off the adrenaline of the last few drills, itching for action. But if they're going to succeed, they've got to learn the mental game.

"This is about reading the ocean, guys. If you can predict what a wave is gonna do, you can be where you need to be when you need to be there," I say, making eye contact with each of them. "This isn't just about reaction; it's about anticipation."

I paddle around them, and they turn to see what I'm going to do. I point out to the horizon where a new set seems to be forming. "See that? You've got to read the wave sets to gauge their speed, their direction, and their shape. Then you decide which wave to catch and how to catch it." As the set rolls in, I make my choice. "Watch and learn."

I start paddling, timing it just right. Just as I feel the wave's energy is about to peak, I pop up and drop in, riding it all the way in a smooth arc right in the pocket. I'm exhilarated when I circle back. I know I made it look easy, and they're looking at me with awe, bordering on hero worship.

"Get what I'm saying? I didn't fight the wave; I used its energy. I was where it wanted me to be," I explain.

Drew nods, his eyes squinting towards the horizon. "I think I see a set," he says before paddling out. He's eager but mistimes his paddling, and the wave passes under him, leaving him behind.

"Too early, Drew. You've got to wait for the right moment," I call out.

Art goes next. He's patient, waiting for his wave. He catches it but misjudges the speed, popping up too late and getting swallowed by the wave's break.

"Close, Art, but you've got to time your pop-up," I coach.

Finally, it's Will's turn. He watches, waits, and then makes his move. Paddling smoothly, he catches the wave at its peak, pops up, and rides it down the line. It's not perfect, but it's the best of the three.

"That's it, Will. You read it right," I shouted, clapping.

As we regroup, I look at each of them. "This is a game of chess, not checkers. It's strategy, timing, and understanding. Are you ready to try again?"

They nod, their faces etched with determination. As they paddle back out, I can see it in their eyes—the realization that surfing isn't just about mastering the water; it's about understanding it.

We spend another hour on the water, each wave a lesson, each ride a step closer to mastery. And as we call it a day, I can't help but think about how much they've grown—not just as surfers, but as people.

Back on the patio, I put my board on the rack, feeling a quiet satisfaction. Not just in what Drew, Will and Art have learned but in what I've remembered— Life, like the ocean, is both unpredictable and beautiful. And the better we get at reading its signs, the better our ride will be. Maybe it was Charlie who told us that, I can't remember, but nonetheless, it's a good motto to remember.

It's Friday night, and Date Night finally rolled around. I stared at myself in the mirror, still wet from the shower, a towel wrapped around my waist. Tonight wasn't about waxing boards or timing waves. Instead, it was about something far more unpredictable: my date with Lara. I slick my hair back, unsure if I should go for the casual, just-off-the-beach look or something a bit more refined. I opt for a last option and brush my hair until it's smooth and shiny, and braid it, spacing silver rings every few inches to keep it in the braid and heavy enough to hang down my back without swinging like a pendulum or flipping over my shoulder.

I foraged through my closet, looking for a crisp button-down and a pair of slacks. The blue shirt looks good with the charcoal gray slacks, and I pull out the leather loafers. I pulled on a thin leather jacket it got a little chilly. I had no idea where we were going, but I would leave it in the truck if I didn't need it. My reflection gives me a nod of approval; my look is appropriate for dinner but still casual. My phone buzzes with a text. It's from Drew. He's in his room down the hall, and I wonder why he's texting me rather than walking the few steps to my door.

"Good luck tonight, coach. Don't screw it up!" It says, with a laughing emoji.

I chuckled. The boys have been teasing me all day. I shoot back a quick *"Thanks, my man."* before pocketing my phone and grabbing my keys.

As I step into my truck, I grin like a teenage boy. It's been a while since I've been on a *date* date, going to pick her up from home and everything. I wonder if I should have bought her some flowers or something.

Lara lived in her own house across town, though I'd thought she stayed at the Inn, either in the apartment with Lily or in one of her own. I pull up in front of her place and take a deep breath, steadying myself. Before I could think too much, I stepped out of the truck, which I had cleaned and detailed until every inch of it gleamed, and headed to her door. I rapped twice on the door, my heart doing its own little drum solo. I feel a different kind of exhilaration waiting for her to answer the knock on her door. I'm not reading waves tonight; I'm navigating emotions, signals, and that age-old dance between two people who are attracted to each other.

And as she opened the door, all thoughts of nerves and apprehension vanished. She is stunning, her smile outshining the setting sun. And just like that, I'm reminded that life isn't just about riding the big waves—it's about enjoying the calm and beautiful moments in between.

The restaurant was named *La Belle Étoile*, and everything about it oozed sophistication. Dim lighting, the mellifluous notes of a jazz saxophone in the background, and the chandeliers cast a warm, golden hue over the dining area. The flicker of candlelight reflected off the pristine white table linens, the ambient murmurs of conversation and the soft clink of China and heavy silverware filled the room, creating an atmosphere that was both intimate and refined.

As Lara and I were ushered to our table by the host, I couldn't help but notice how radiant she looked. The soft candlelight highlighted her features, making her eyes flicker with a particular sparkle. "Incredible choice, Lara," I commented, taking in the surroundings with an appreciative glance.

"Only the best for our celebration." She laughed softly, her eyes meeting mine.

Our waiter, a polished guy in his late 40s, approached our table and extended his menus. "Bonsoir."

I catch Lara's eye as I respond, "Bonsoir, merci." She hid her big grin by rolling her lips in between her teeth and clamping down on them. She looked both surprised and pleased.

"Le chef a-t-il des recommandations pour le dîner de ce soir?"

"Oui monsieur, voici nos plats vedettes de ce soir." He handed us two smaller menus, hand-written in a spidery script.

When the waiter left us to peruse the menus, she leaned forward. "You said you loved French food. You didn't mention you also spoke French."

"A few stints a year in and around Biarritz, France, when I was on the circuit," I explain. "Picked up a little French along the way, just enough to get by."

"Still, I'm impressed," she says, grinning. "What did you say? I can't speak or read a word of it."

"I asked him if the chef had any recommendations for tonight's dinner, and he said yes and handed us the specials menu."

The waiter returned to discuss the wine list, turning his attention to me. "Monsieur, Mademoiselle, puis-je vous suggérer un vin?"

"Un Sancerre serait parfait, je pense," I suggest, giving Lara a quick glance for approval.

"Excellente choix, Monsieur," the waiter says before departing. I caught Lara looking at me when I glanced over at her, and I began to laugh. I liked the way she was smiling at me.

"This menu is a culinary tour de France. I remember you saying you like the *Duck à l'Orange*."

She chuckled. "I do. But I'd like to try something different. Will you order for me?"

"Absolutely. Let's see. How about the 'Chateaubriand pour deux'? I hope it's prepared tableside. You'd love it."

"Okay," she says happily. "Will you tell me what it is?"

"Nope. But I'll bet you recognize it when it comes. As for

an appetizer, let's start with the Charcuterie board." She agreed, and I gave the waiter our order.

As we started with the variety of artisanal cheeses and cured meats, our conversation ebbed and flowed. Lara wanted to know everything from my travel escapades to my favorite hole-in-the-wall joints in far-flung places. Conversing with her was effortless, like long-lost friends catching up, far removed from the constructs of a *first date*.

When the Chateaubriand arrived, the waiter ceremoniously flambéed it right in front of us. The expression on Lara's face was priceless. But better than that was the taste—ah, the taste was Magnifique.

"Qu'en pensez-vous?" I asked her in French, then again in English.

"It's extraordinary," she replies, her eyes meeting mine.

We shared a Tarte Tatin for dessert, the caramelized apples melding perfectly with the flaky crust. It's the kind of dessert that makes you wish you had a second stomach.

"Merci pour cette soirée merveilleuse, Lara. Merci d'être sorti avec moi, et de m'avoir offert une belle maison," I said, genuinely pleased by the evening.

"What does that mean?" She asks, resting her chin in her palm, supporting it with an elbow on the table.

"Thank you for this wonderful evening. Thank you for coming out with me and for giving me a beautiful house.

"You are very welcome for all three." She laughed.

The waiter brought out our check, and I quickly intercepted

it before Lara could grab it. I signed it and handed him my credit card. Over a fresh glass of wine, our conversation continued to flow.

"You know," Lara started, taking a sip from her crystal wine glass, "when you first approached me with the house project, I thought you'd be just another out-of-towner, but now, it feels like I've known you for years."

I leaned forward, captivated. "I feel the same way. We seemed to have had a connection from the beginning."

She blushed, her fingers playing with the silverware. "I never expected that, but I'm glad it happened." I smiled, and we toasted to friendship, clinking our crystal wine goblet together.

The evening progressed, and the boundaries of client and contractor had long been blurred. Now, it felt like two people rediscovering each other. At one point, our hands brushed against each other, sending a jolt of electricity up my spine. I took a chance, entwining my fingers with hers. She looked up, surprise evident in her eyes, but she didn't pull away. We continued to chat, laugh, and flirt, the world outside fading into insignificance. It was just us, two people connecting over candlelight, drawn together by providence.

CHAPTER ELEVEN

I woke up earlier than usual and got dressed quickly.

I let the boys sleep in because I needed to focus on something else this morning. Today was Cal's one day to surf. The lumberyard opened later on Sundays than during the rest of the week, and Cal never missed the opportunity to get in a couple of hours on the water. The morning sun was still a pale white light, casting glimmers on the vast expanse of the ocean when I took the cliffside steps down to the beach. It was still early, and there were few people out and about. But last night, I'd talked to my friends, Alec Townsend and James Russell, who had just arrived in town and were settling in at Lily's and asked them to meet me on the beach at seven.

We'd been good friends for over a decade, and I trusted their judgment. They were experienced and savvy talent management agents with two of the biggest agencies around, and Josh, Colin and I had worked with them for years, securing many of the huge sponsor endorsements we represented on the circuit through them. Seeing them in the distance, I jogged over to them. It was good to see them again.

"I hope this kid you've been raving about lives up to the hype, Sean," Alec remarked, a teasing tone in his voice.

I smiled. "Just watch."

I looked for Cal and saw him carry his board into the water. The sun broke through a cloud just as he began to paddle out, and it seemed that even God and all of the Angels wanted to see him clearly. Moments later, he was in position, but he seemed to settle in and wait. He waited for what seemed like eons before exploding with controlled energy and taking on a monster wave. It was thrilling to watch him ride the crest with unparalleled elegance, his board poetry in motion. He executed a series of tricks with such power and grace he made my friends' jaws drop. I even heard them audibly gasp as he executed a particularly audacious aerial move with more finesse than most veterans could, and Jim gave me an approving nod.

Cal took several more waves, but neither Alec nor Jim complained as we watched, spellbound. When he emerged from a tunnel, the wave crashing behind him in a frothy explosion, both Alec and Jim cheered, clapping each other and me on the back. I couldn't help grinning ear to ear.

Jim turned to me, his eyes wide. "He's incredible. Has he been sponsored yet?"

I shook my head, excited that they were so impressed. "Not yet, but with that kind of talent, I'm hoping he won't be unsponsored for long."

"Man, Sean. I didn't believe you when you told me he was something special. A nineteen-year-old kid surfing like that? Who trained him?"

"I'm not sure. Cal told me his uncle taught him, but he learned a lot on his own, watching other surfers. Look, here he comes."

I watched Call approach us, a tentative smile on his face. Still grinning from ear to ear, I gave him two thumbs up. His face broke out in the sunniest, happiest expression imaginable.

"Cal, I'd like you to meet my friends Alec and Jim. Gentlemen, Calvin Easton." The men shook his hand, and both began talking excitedly at the same time. I stood to the side, watched Cal, and smiled even harder as I saw that he was momentarily at a loss for words as the men practically bombarded him with questions about his training and his future. He looked back at me, and I nodded encouragingly. I watched as Alec and Jim congratulated Cal, feeling exceptionally proud of him, and I slipped away to make a call.

"Hey, it's me!" I said as soon as Josh answered.

"Hey, Dude. What's Up?"

"You won't believe what just happened!" I could barely contain my excitement.

He laughed, "You sound like you've won the lottery or something. What's going on?"

"Remember Cal? The kid I told you and Charlie about?" I started pacing the sandy shore, my footsteps leaving imprints that mirrored the whirlwind of emotions inside me.

"Yeah, of course. The prodigy surfer. What about him?"

"Alec Townsend and Jim Russell drove up today and watched him surf, and they were blown away, man! Like, seriously impressed!" My voice rose in pitch with every word.

There was a moment of stunned silence before Josh whooped into the phone.

"No way! That's massive, dude! I knew he was that good. This is going to be next level for him!"

"I know! I can't believe it. I mean, I believed in him, but to see him get this kind of response in Alec and Jim? It's just... insane!" I took a deep breath, trying to process it all.

Josh's voice softened, "You did good, Sean, not just for Cal, but for yourself. You've turned your passion into something that's changing lives. I'm proud of you, man."

I chuckled, brushing away the hint of moisture from my eyes. "Thanks, Bro. That means a lot. I wanted to share the good news with you."

"Yeah, of course. Glad you did. I've got a doctor's appointment this morning and can't be late. Call me later, okay?"

"Yeah, sure, but what kind of doctor? Cassidy?"

"Nah. Plastic surgeon. He's going to work on my leg."

"Really? That's awesome."

"Yeah, it is. Now, go celebrate with Cal. This is just the beginning for him. He's going to need a friend he can trust."

As I ended the call, I looked out at the ocean. Today wasn't just another day at the beach; it was the beginning of something bigger.

That evening, after the boys left for their evening practice, I sent Lara a text, asking if she'd like to go somewhere to listen to some music and grab a bite to eat and a beer. Her response was almost instantaneous. *Heck Yeah.*

When's good for you? I shot back.

Can I get an hour? Just a few things to wrap up before I can get away. I can meet you somewhere.

An hour's fine. You choose the place? I'm not familiar with bars here. I've only seen the one down from your grandmother on High Street.

I think we can find somewhere nicer than that. I'll pick you up.

Okay. Text me when you're on your way.

Will do. I smiled at the turn of things, and I liked the idea of Lara coming to pick me up for a date. Things felt very uncomplicated between us. No drama.

Lara arrived an hour later, but to my surprise, she handed me a hamper of food and carried a pack of Cooper Premiums. "Whatever's in here," I said, sniffing the top of the hamper, "smells absolutely delicious."

"I figured your place was nicer than a bar and grill."

"Oo-kay. To the patio?"

"Please."

I happily carried the food through the garden and around to the back of the house and set it on a dining chair. Setting the beer down, Lara wiped the top of the cocktail table sitting in front of the two-seater sofa with a paper towel and spread a linen napkin. I brought the hamper over and watched as she brought out bread and meat, stuffed mussels, fried squid, sautéed mushrooms, kalamata olives, and other vegetables. It was a feast, with cold beers to wash it all down. After setting out the buffet, she plugged her phone into the speaker system, and relaxing instrumentals filled the air. I was properly impressed. She was right. It was much nicer than any bar and grill we could have found.

Making myself useful, I lit a fire in the pit, more for ambiance and to keep away the flying insects than to provide heat, as the temperatures still hovered in the seventies.

We ate and listened to the music and the fire popping and snapping as the logs burned and enjoyed the stillness of the evening. The ocean below was a dark abyss, inky and vast, except where moonlight broke through thick, scudding clouds drifting across the night sky and spilled a line of liquid silver that shimmered on the waves. It was hauntingly beautiful.

The fire flared up, casting a warm, flickering glow on Lara's face. Not for the first time, I was caught up in how lovely she was. She was beautiful, with her large, luminous blue eyes, wheat-blonde hair, and mischievous smile, but her beauty was more than just her physical appearance. I found her confidence, intelligence, independence, and strength of character made her beautiful, as did her openness, honesty, empathy and great sense of humor appealing. She looked up at me, catching me staring.

"What?" she asked, her lips curling into that smile that always made my heart skip a beat.

"Nothing," I said, looking away briefly, then back into her eyes. "Just thinking how perfect this is."

She leaned in closer, her hand snaking around my bicep and giving me a hug. "It is perfect, isn't it. You didn't let me treat you to dinner at *La Belle Etoile*. I was supposed to be my treat, remember?"

"I do, and you did. Choosing that place was more than a treat." I picked up her hand lying on my arm with my free one and cradled it. Her eyes sparkled, reflecting the flames, and she squeezed my arm.

"So, what are your plans after this competition wraps up and summer is over?"

"Nose to the grindstone, I suppose. I need to get back to work, especially after that chunk you took out of my bank account," I said teasingly before taking a sip of my beer. "I've been thinking of going back to work for Brenner Industrials. I took a long lunch break that lasted fifteen, maybe sixteen years, to go surfing with Josh. I'm hoping they're still holding my position, or maybe they'll give me a little bump up if I could get Josh to come back too."

"Seriously? A lunch break fifteen years long? To go surfing?"

"Yeah. Josh and I thought it would be fun."

"Was it?"

"Yeah, it was…until it wasn't."

A memory of the shark attack that took Colin and nearly took Josh, too, popped into my mind, and I suppose it did in hers as well. The sparkle that usually filled her eyes dimmed, and she tightened her arm on mine. A profound sadness settled between us, and I suddenly gave in to the urge that I'd been repressing for months. I leaned in, my lips just a breath away from hers, and when she didn't pull away, I kissed her. Softly. Lingeringly. Filled with promise. But as I pulled back, something shifted in her eyes. A hesitation.

"I need to tell you something, Sean," she said, her grip on

my arm loosening.

"Okay, what's up?" I asked, feeling a knot tighten in my stomach. It didn't sound like good news. I immediately wondered if she had a significant other—a husband or maybe a wife—tucked away at home. I knew it was a crass thought, but there it was. I waited quietly for her to speak, watching her as she looked down, taking a deep breath as if steeling herself.

"I really like you, Sean, I do, but my dream of building my own business is taking off, finally, and I'm committed to Lily— they're my top priorities right now. Lily is my only family. I can't leave her."Her words hang in the air, each one landing like a quiet thud in my chest, but at least there was no one else. I searched her eyes, trying to gauge how difficult this was for her to say.

"I get it, Lara. Truly, I do."

"You do?" Her eyes meet mine, searching for sincerity.

"Yeah," I say, squeezing her hand gently, ignoring the sharp pang of disappointment in my chest that threatened to move up into my throat and choke me. "Your dreams, your family— they're part of what makes you, you. I wouldn't want to come between that."

She exhaled, the tension visibly leaving her body. "You're one of the good ones, you know?"

I gave her a half-smile, feeling a strange mix of relief and loss, and taking up her hand again, I gave it a squeeze.

"If you say so. But what I do know for sure is that Carmichael is a good place to live. Lots of good people here that look after each other," I say, trying to fill the silence and lighten the mood.

"It has that effect on people," she replied, smiling softly. "But it's not Sydney, is it?"

I shake my head. "No, it's not. It has it's own charm, though. It's been relaxing being here, but there's not much for me to do. I should have been back home weeks ago, but I want to stay until after the competition. I just needed some time to get my head back on right."

"And I've got my contracting business here. It's been a long time, but it's finally taking off, and I can't leave Carmichael. Not now. Probably not ever."

We looked at one another, and the undeniable chemistry, the shared laughs, the mutual respect—it was all still there, but so were the realities of our separate lives, pulling us in opposite directions.

"Sometimes... sometimes the timing isn't right," She unwound her arm from around mine and instead of letting go, she intertwined her fingers with mine, her thumb running over the back of my hand in slow circles as if trying to soften the edges of her words.

"I understand timing," I reply, my gaze drifting from our hands back to her eyes. "And ambition, and passion for what one does and wants."

She smiles at me, but it's tinged with a sadness I haven't seen before. "You're so understanding, Sean."

I give her a reassuring squeeze, my fingers tightening around hers for just a moment.

"I try," I said, setting her hand down on the arm of her chair and picking our beers from where we'd set them on the patio floor beside our chairs. I handed her bottle to her and clinked mine against it.

"Life is too short for regrets, Lara. So don't regret what we don't have. Celebrate what we do have. If it's friendship, then it's friendship. It's still more than most people have in a lifetime."

I probably should have stood up and made that toast, I thought to myself. I sounded very grandiose even sitting down. Lara grinned at me, apparently thinking the same thing, and we took a long swallow of our beer.

"Thank you, Sean." She said after getting her smile under control. "You have no idea how much I needed to hear that." She laid her head on my shoulder, and though it was a small gesture, it felt huge, a testament to the emotional whirlwind that we'd just experienced. Silence enveloped us, but it was a comfortable one this time, filled with a newfound understanding. We both knew the landscape had shifted beneath us, but there was also a tacit agreement that it was a landscape still worth exploring, even if the path forward was now different.

CHAPTER
TWELVE

We had about a week and a half before Opening Day, and the town was already inundated with visitors.

The energy around town was palpable. Tourists, having heard about the competition, flocked to Carmichael in droves, their enthusiasm evident in their wide-eyed wonder and animated chatter. Everywhere I went, from the grocery store to the beach front cafes, conversations buzzed about the upcoming event. The beach, once a serene haven, had transformed into a bustling hive of activity. Temporary structures sprouted up overnight, designed to accommodate the crowds of spectators expected to attend. Large platforms with covered seating areas offered prime views of the action, while tents and umbrellas being anchored in the sand let enthusiasts feel closer to the action. Every lamppost and billboard seemed to sport banners of the competition's sponsors, their bright colors snapping in the sea breeze.

Perhaps most noticeable was the extensive presence of the media. Along the beach front and along High Street, production crews worked tirelessly, setting up their equipment and ensuring every angle of the competition and a lot of interesting human interest stories could be captured. I spotted the unmistakable logos of ESPN, SuperSport, Sky News, BSI, ISB, and others on more than one van around town, a clear indication of how big this event had become. There were also dozens of luxury RVs and campers everywhere, lining the streets and parked in lots and fields, everyone trying to get as close to the beach front as possible. Families, groups of friends, and solo travelers had all converged on the small, quiet town, turning it into a veritable campground. The smell of shrimp, fish, and meat on the grills wafted through the air, and music and laughter echoed well into the night. Walking through town, I overheard snippets of conversation.

"Did you see the line-up of surfers?" one excited voice exclaimed.

"I've never seen anything like this in our town," marveled another.

Locals exchanged stories of previous competitions they'd seen in Spenser and Mercy, but there was unanimous agreement: this year, it was going to be bigger and more thrilling than any of the others held anywhere else. Owners of the local surf shops were making money hand over fist from customers wanting souvenir beach gear and *Big Wave* commemorative T-shirts; restaurants overflowed with hungry patrons; and hotels, motels, and B&Bs boasted No Vacancy signs. The town pulsed with a vibrant energy, a collective eagerness for the competition to begin.

Getting out early Saturday morning, wanting to stretch my legs along the beach and see all the changes taking place, I saw so many surfers, most around Drew, Art and Will's age, out examining the waves and mentally preparing for the challenge ahead. But there were also some older, familiar faces, surfers that I'd known and surfed against for years.

Michael Davis, one such fellow competitor and good friend, called out to me, and I turned to see him jogging toward me.

"Sean! What are you doing here, Man? I thought you were still in the States. How've you been?"

"Good, good. Mike. I've been home about five or six months now. I happened upon the news of this tourney and decided to have a look. How have you been? What are you doing out here?"

"I work for Wavecrest Talent Management. We have a few young surfers participating in the Big Wave competition. How about you?"

"My nephew and his friends came down to try out their water wings. I'm here with them.

"You're doing some training now?"

"Nope, vacationing. But you've been good?"

"I have. Every day's a blessing. I heard about Josh and Colin. Man, I'm so sorry that happened. How's Josh doing?"

"Better. He's back home, too."

"That's awesome. So, man, how long have you been here? You still live in Sydney, right? I thought this was going to be some little jumped-up affair, but these people got some real money backing them. It's going to be epic!"

I laughed, clapping him on the back, not even attempting to answer his stream of questions. "It's going to be a competition for the books, that's for sure."

We chatted for a few minutes more, then I continued down the beach. Everywhere I looked, clusters of surfers were gathered, discussing strategies, sharing insights, and even playfully teasing one another. I even saw groups of teenage boys rough-housing with each other. The young ones always had too much energy to relax before taking their turns. I remembered my early days, the butterflies in my stomach and puking my guts out before a big competition. It had taken years for me to learn how to channel that energy.

Standing on the beach, surrounded by people who loved the sport as much as I did, I felt a deep connection to them, united by the waves, the thrill, and the passion for the sport. I was glad I was here. The competition was going to be fierce, and there were naturally going to be challenges, triumphs, and lessons for the novices to face and overcome. It made me proud that Drew was here, wanting to walk in my shoes.

When I returned home later that afternoon, I found Drew, Art, and Will avidly watching the news on the television,

"Uncle Sean. Have you heard the news?" Drew asked without looking at me, which made me feel something was terribly wrong.

"No. What is it?" I went over to sit next to them to see what they were looking at. A forecaster was sharing the latest weather update, and there appeared to be a massive cyclone heading straight for our coast, promising extreme wind and rain. I shook my head, my heart already sinking with a sense of foreboding. The room was thick with tension, each of us hanging on the weatherman's every word.

"What about the competition this week?"

"I don't know. If it hits us Sunday night and lasts through Tuesday morning, as they're predicting, it may give us time to clean up on Wednesday. Hopefully, if it delays the competition, it may only be for a day or two, depending on how much damage it causes." I said, hoping to sound encouraging. The boys, however, continued to look glum.

After a few hours of hanging around the house watching the news, I hustled them into my truck and drove down to Lindy's Lumberyard to meet Lara, who was helping to organize residents and visitors into volunteer teams. I knew our help boarding up homes and businesses, running back and forth to make sure everyone had enough food and supplies to ride out the storm, and ensuring everyone would be safe would be welcome. We worked well into the night, securing as many properties as we could.

Saturday morning, we were out again, this time stripping the spectator stands and vendor booths down to the scaffolding frames. I was exhausted when we finished for the day, more than ready to sit down, put my feet up and watch the weather channel track tropical depression Leslie.

I was starting to nod off when I heard a truck pull up in front of the house and loud voices. A truckload of construction workers and neighbors had arrived at our house, ready to help us move the outdoor furniture into the garage, including the front porch swing with chain links as thick as my fist, and cover the brand-new windows and glass French doors with boards. I'd naively believed my house was safe, nestled as it was in a little cranny on the cliff. It had stood for generations of Hendersons without blowing off, and Lara and her crew had just finished reinforcing it from the foundation to the roof a scant few weeks ago. Lara was standing on the porch when I answered the pounding she'd given my door with her fist.

"We've come to board up your baby, Sean Hargrove. I'll not see all my hard work blown over your fields." I grinned at her and stepped aside. One person followed her in while a half-dozen or so more people began dragging sheets of wood, hammers and nails to the ground-floor windows.

Once the house was secure and the workers were gone, I stood on the balcony overlooking the ocean and stared at the darkening sky, gripping the railings against the fury of Leslie. The storm was still out in the Pacific, but the waves were already crashing higher and angrier onto the shore, and seagulls and other birds, usually so brazen, were long gone. The wind was a harsh, biting force that made the towering palm trees bow and sway as if in prayer.

"Are you okay out here, Uncle?" Drew, who had been in the garden and had come around to the back, shouted above the wail of the wind.

"I'm fine. Don't worry. I'll be up in a minute," I yelled over the rising wind, my voice barely audible above the approaching fury. With determination, I stood defiantly at the railing, the ocean stretching out before me, a fierce beast awakening. Lightning flashed in the distance, illuminating the churning waves beneath the brooding sky. I wiped my brow with the back of my hand, smearing a mixture of sweat and sea mist across my face. The relentless gusts snatched at my clothing as if nature itself was trying to undress me. Unfazed, I tugged my shirt over my head, exposing my bare chest to the elements. My skin prickled from the biting chill and the relentless mist that clung to me like a blanket.

The ocean's tumultuous rumble mingled with the thunderous percussion of the storm's thunder and lightning. My hair, once neatly braided, danced wildly in the tempest, long strands breaking free and whipping around me like cat-o'-nine-tails. In that moment, as the world around me succumbed to the darkness and wildness of the storm, I stood as a solitary figure, a defiant soul in the face of nature's fury. The wild tides and I met in a stand-off of power and vulnerability, each daring the other to yield.

~

I pulled my phone out and read a text that came in from Lizzie.

We've heard the weather forecast for up that way. We have beautiful weather here, but it seems like a big storm's heading your way. How bad is it up there? We're ready to drive up on Wednesday.

My fingers hovered over the screen, then I responded. *Waiting for it to hit sometime overnight or early in the morning.*

Hopefully, it will have moved on by Wednesday, and we'll have a good idea of how much damage it caused. It could delay everything.

She texted back, *Keep in touch. We'll come once it's safe, even if there's no competition. It shouldn't take us more than eight or ten hours, depending on traffic heading that way.*

I'd given Lizzie a call last weekend and filled her in on everything, including where I was, what I had done, and the fact that Drew was up here with me. We'd talked a long time during that call, and I believed I'd convinced her and Mom not to worry or be too upset with Drew. At least he was safe with me. I also told her that I'd made a deal with him to return to school if things didn't go the way he had planned. She had sputtered and spit before finally promising me. I invited her, Mom, and the boys up to watch Drew surf in the competition, without his knowledge, of course, and enjoy a holiday with us. She and Mom had immediately started making plans to drive up a few days ahead of opening Day so they could spend some time with Drew before the competition began. Now, however, I wanted them to wait before making the drive. It also looked like the Amateur competition might be delayed by the storm.

Henry Hayes, a carpenter who had worked on the house with Lara earlier this month, must have seen me or heard me and Drew talking and also came around to the patio. Deciding to join me, he came up the stairs to the balcony and looked around before coming to stand at the railing beside me. I felt a strange unity with him, this impending disaster reminding me of the fragility of humankind and that our strength could—and should—come from the deep-rooted strength we shared as a whole. I remained quiet as he took in the view from every direction.

"You have the perfect sightline for watching the storm roll in," he finally said.

"Yeah. But I had only wanted to watch the competition from here, not a freaking cyclone."

He nodded, then after a long minute, he said, "Guess it's go-time." I looked up as the first raindrops began to fall like little liquid drumbeats heralding the arrival of the storm.

"Yeah, let's get inside."

"I'm going to get back to town and the family. I need to make sure they stay calm."

"Alright," I said, raising my hand in a wave. I waited to see Henry make it back down the stairs. Then I took a deep breath, savoring the electrified air, before going back inside.

Sunday night was surreal. I'd opted in for weather alerts on my mobile phone, and it seemed to buzz every few minutes. I glanced at the screen, but I was already aware of what the message had to say, as I was also glued to the television screen. The National Weather Service had upgraded Leslie from a severe tropical depression to a potential cyclone. I stood up from the sofa and walked over to the front door. Opening it, I looked up at the sky. Ominous, bruise-colored clouds, whipped by strong winds, had amassed, turning the sky into a massive, swirling canvas of grays and blacks. The air felt charged with electricity and muggy, like a wet blanket weighing on me. I could hear the wind battering the headlands and the waves heaving and crashing against the shore behind the house. I felt my stomach tighten. This was going to be bad, I thought, real bad.

The ancient oak trees that had stood in the yard for ages started swaying more vigorously, their leaves rustling like whispered warnings from Mother Nature herself. I swiped my screen for more information—high winds, flash floods, dangerous swells. If this storm was half as bad as the weather reports predicted, maybe we should have evacuated instead of boarding everything up. I was responsible not just for myself but for Drew, Art, and Will. Instead of staying at the house, maybe we should have driven over to one of the other nearby towns a little further inland. I might have been a bit foolish, thinking we would be safe in this house in conditions like this. My fingers tightened around my phone. We'd done everything I could think of to ride this storm out, and I resigned myself to the fact that it was probably too late to get in the truck and find somewhere else to stay the night.

It was late, and my brain was mush after watching the weather channel all evening, so I decided to go upstairs, lay down, and get a little shuteye. I lay across my bed, but I'm hyper-aware of every noise outside the house. The storm has slowly been ratcheting up, the rain a staccato drum beat against the roof, the flickers of lightning like a flashbulb capturing a moment of impending chaos, the wind gusting and swirling, picking up anything it can and smashing it against any obstacle in its way.

I've never been afraid of storms before, no matter how intense they became, and I've experienced every weather phenomenon in every country for more than a decade—volcanic eruptions that shut down competitions and forced us off the host islands, strong earthquakes that lasted minutes rather than mere seconds; and dozens of tropical depressions that turned into cyclones and vice versa. I've experienced all manner of weather and natural events traveling around the world, and never once have I ever feared for my life. But tonight, it wasn't just me I had to worry about. There were three young men on the precipice of their lives locked up in this house with me.

We shouldn't have stayed, reverberated in my brain. *I should've packed up the guys and got them to someplace a lot safer.* That thought began to race around in my head, and I had to shake it off forcefully.

I stopped by the second-floor guest rooms to check on Drew, Art and Will. They were knocked out, oblivious to the storm outside. Apparently, the wind howling like a pack of ravening wolves outside their windows and gusts slamming into the house as if testing the integrity of each nail, each plank of wood, was not enough to disturb their slumber. I closed their doors behind me and continued to my room, intending to lie down, but once inside, I walked over to the boarded-up French doors that led to the balcony. I tried the knobs, but they were boarded up and secured from the outside against the wind, rain, and any debris coming off the ocean and the beach below.

I was too restless to go to bed, so I turned around and went back downstairs. A hot drink might take the edge off, and I enter the kitchen, fill the kettle, and put it on the stove, only to realize

I don't really want a cup of tea. A single stubby of Cooper Premium, left over from the evening with Lara, was in the fridge, and I grabbed that instead. I carried it back to the sofa, where I'd been all evening and turned the TV back on. As I sipped my beer and surfed television channels, a monstrous gust of wind suddenly smacked the house. The whole structure shudders, and for a moment, I swear I heard the house groan in protest. I wait to see if any other noise occurs, but the house seems to settle down, so I try to as well.

It rained heavily, steadily, for more than thirty hours, a hard drenching rain that pooled on paved streets and flooded outlying areas.

CHAPTER THIRTEEN

I woke up to the sound of birds chirping, a stark contrast to last night's howling winds and relentless rain.

The morning sun was streaming through the curtains, painting the room in a warm golden glow; the sky was a clear blue, not a cloud in sight. And I sat up and immediately reached for my phone—no messages, no emergency alerts. That was a good sign, but I needed to see the aftermath of Cyclone Leslie for myself.

I jumped out of bed and threw on some clothes. A glance out of the window revealed branches scattered about but nothing catastrophic. Still, I had to see what had happened in the town center, where buildings were older and more susceptible to damage. I couldn't believe our luck. At the last minute, like a shy performer, Leslie changed course, sparring the town the worst of its wrath and leaving only minor damage in her wake before dissipating more than twenty-four hours after making landfall. The most we'd received was the deluge of rain and strong winds that ripped away loose bits of siding, roofing, tree limbs, small branches, and other debris. Nothing I hoped would take more than a few days to clean up. Some of the damaged houses might need a week or more, but fortunately, no one got hurt or lost their life.

I ran into Lily outside her café and Inn, and I was surprised. I think it was the first time I'd ever seen her from behind her reception desk. Lily was standing outside with Lara, looking over the façade of her building. I don't know what seemed to be worrying the two women, but I didn't see any damage or anything out of place, for that matter.

"Good morning, ladies. We were lucky, weren't we?"

"Oh, Sean. We were. How did you and your nephews cope out there on the cliffs?"

"We were tucked in, but I think my nephews have eaten everything there was to eat. I'm sure they'll be coming down here to clean your out as well."

"Oh, I'm ready for them," she said, chuckling. "Well, I guess I should go in and help in the dining room. We're filled to the rafters but don't mind me. I'm over the moon about it."

I gave Lily a hug before she went inside and turned to Lara. "What are you up to this morning, Ms. Finnegan?"

"We've been helping take down boards now that the storm has moved up the coast. I came by to make sure the boards were down over here. I asked Stuart to take the ones off Grams' windows first. How about you?"

"I wanted to see the damage for myself."

"Well, come walk with me for a bit."

"Okay, but let me get a coffee first. Do you want one?"

"Yes, thank you."

I got VIP service. Lily brought back two to-go cups of coffee and two breakfast pastries for me. I gave her a peck on the cheek and hurried back to where Lara was waiting. She walked beside me, dressed in her overalls, and her hair scraped back into her usual ponytail. But her eyes seemed to scan everything everywhere, and I could see they were filled with astonishment and relief. Others joined us, their faces also etched with a mix of wonder and gratitude. I imagined we made a surreal sight walking down the middle of High Street and people coming from every direction to join us. An older woman saw Lara at the head of the procession and hurried over to clasp her hand. Her voice trembled with amazement, her words escaping in a hushed tone, "Can you believe it, Lara? It's like a miracle that the storm decided to change direction. It was a miracle."

Lara nodded, "I was so worried. It's incredible how things can change in the blink of an eye. It'll be easy to get all this debris cleaned up," she said, pointing to branches strewn down the street. It was a far cry from the devastation we had feared.

"Well, Opening Day just might open on schedule," I leaned sideways and murmured.

Her eyes sparkled with excitement as she responded.

"I know, right?!! We still have our chance to shine. Cyclone Leslie may have thrown us a curveball, but we're still in the game."

The crowd and I followed Lara as she turned toward the beach. A group of men, and there had to be more than a hundred, most of them were surfers, were standing in front of a makeshift platform listening to Miles Sturdivant, the production coordinator from the event production company, give them directions. As I approached, I could hear him speaking into the mic.

"Alright, team, The medical authorities advised that everyone stay out of the water for at least twenty-four to thirty-six hours. In the meantime, we'll divide and conquer. We need a lot of eyes on the beach. We'll split up into two teams, one for structural checks and the other to handle debris. We need to get the beach back into pristine condition. Mayor Bailey, can we count on the town council to get the results on water quality?"

Mayor Clive Bailey, a robust man with a permanent tan, raised his hand and nodded. "Consider it done, Mr. Sturdivant. We'll expedite the tests and have results back in 48 hours, max."

Miles nodded, and the group cheered. Many of the folks who'd come down with Lara, myself included, joined the first group and then split up into the two smaller teams, while some others went back to the town center. I joined the debris team, and armed with gloves and trash bags, I headed to the beach with the other volunteers. Thankfully, it was mostly seaweed and driftwood and a bit of plastic, nothing a strong pair of hands couldn't handle.

"Alright, folks! Debris team, you're with Jake Harris right over here. Structural integrity, you're with Georgie Crocker and Mr. Henry Hayes, two of our best carpenters, right over here."

I smiled at Henry and joined the large party of men and women already armed with vinyl gloves and trash bags. We fanned out across the beach, bagging everything on the beach.

"It's freakin' unbelievable, man, that we dodged that cyclone!" said a younger man who was obviously not a resident of the town. His voice tinged with awe and disbelief.

I chuckle, sharing the sentiment. "I think Mother Nature

loves surfers," I say, stopping to pick up a couple of pieces of driftwood and seaweed lying half-buried in the sand. "But I think it's going to be a lot of work to get the town back in shape for Opening Day."

Carrying a full bag of debris, I head back to the makeshift stand where a trash collector is sitting. People are handing their bags to the operator, who empties them into a large container. When it was full, he climbed inside the truck cab, pulled the container onto the back of the truck, and hauled it off. The next truck in line pulled up, and the process repeated itself. As I handed the truck driver my bag, I saw Henry walk by.

"How's it going, Henry?" I asked, catching up to him.

"I don't like the look of that platform," Henry mumbled and shook his head. When we stopped in front of one of the struts holding up the judges' platform, he began to shake it, testing it with his hands.

"No way this will hold up when the judges start jumping around, excited about someone's awesome aerial."

I can't help but smile at his remark. The man seemed to know his surf moves as well as he knew carpentry.

"You're here to help me?" He asked, turning to look at me.

"I can," I said hesitantly. "I was just finishing up on the debris team, and I heard you talking to yourself over here. What do you need me to do?"

"We're going to need a few more hands over here. Guys that know how to use a power drill."

"I can hammer some nails, but I don't trust anything I put

together with a power drill."

Henry laughed and clasped me on the shoulder. "I wasn't going to say it, but I was thinking the same thing, Sean. But, if you want to lend a hand, you can sand down these edges. The last thing we need is for people to get a bunch of splinters."

The day goes by pretty fast, and it's early evening before I realize it. I have worked on dozens of tasks that seem small but are crucial to the event's success. By the end of the day—at least for me, we have transformed the beach into something that looks less like a storm's afterthought and more like a competition venue. My stomach is completely empty. I can't remember if I had eaten anything since coffee and pastries this morning with Lily. I doubt it from the sounds coming from my belly.

Every day, I came out to help clean up. Drew, Art and Will would sometimes accompany me, but mostly, I came by myself, getting up and out before they even woke up. I arrived on the beach, and Mayor Bailey and several town council members were already there. The mayor was pacing back and forth near the registration booth, red-faced and yelling into his mobile phone.

"I don't care what you need to do; I need those water test results ASAP. This event brings in tourists, revenue, and a heck of a good time. Don't you screw this up, Lambert!"

When he hung up, Miles was there, waiting to find out what was going on. "Everything alright, Mayor?"

Bailey sighs, visibly stressed. "Water quality is taking longer than expected. But we should have it in a few hours. It wasn't too bad yesterday."

Miles nodded and smiled encouragingly, understanding the weight of the Mayor's responsibility. "Well, in the meantime, Ladies and Gents," he says, turning to the rest of us standing around. "Let's get the competitor zones marked and all of the signs up."

We got to work with the spray paint cans, wooden stakes, ropes, and big poster signs that Miles handed out. While I'd never done any of this, I was familiar with the purpose of it, that being it was crucial to designate where competitors should be before their heats, not just for the organization but for safety.

"Hey, watch it!" Miles yelled. "That line's more crooked than a politician." We all laughed as one of the younger volunteers sprayed a wiggly boundary line. Miles and an older volunteer helped the young man make the correction.

"Straight lines, my man. Just imagine you're riding a perfect wave. Smooth and straight until you hit the lip and launch that air reverse!"

We laugh again, but the young volunteer nods, clearly motivated by the older volunteer, who was obviously a long-time surfer and had perfected his lines. By mid-morning, all of the competitor zones are perfectly outlined.

The next day, Officer Nash cleared the beach so he and the other officers could perform a safety check. I was asked to accompany him through the event space, and I am as curious as he is.

"Can't say it often enough: safety's not a joke," he intoned as he scrutinized the medical tent, his eyes sharp behind dark sunglasses.

"We've got first aid kits, defibrillators, and a hotline to the nearest hospital," I say, reading from the list Miles has given me.

"Good, good," Nash mutters, then points at the fire extinguishers near the food stalls. "Those up to code?"

"They are. Miles double and triple-checked them himself."

Nash grunts approvingly. "Alright, carry on."

We finally conclude the safety inspection, Nash having pried and poked into every nook, cranny, and anthill he could find. He signed off on the certificate beneath the list I'd read from, and I turned it over to Miles, who picked up the mic and made an announcement.

"Safety checks out, people. Good work all around!" Everyone on the beach cheers, and I feel a wave of relief wash over me. The sun is beginning to set, casting golden hues over the ocean, and I'm dog-tired. We've been working nonstop since before the storm, and I'm pretty exhausted. I think a couple shots of Jameson and a long nap are in order, so I trudge through the sand to the stairs that scale the rockface to the house and start to climb. However, it's the thought of taking a hot shower first that keeps me putting one foot in front of the other.

CHAPTER FOURTEEN

Thursday morning, I dressed and hurried over to the beach, where guys were gathering to be assigned to work teams.

The grandstands needed some final touch-ups. The PA system needed testing. And the competitor area needed to be re-set. Always a competitor, I never realized how much work went into setting up a competition so that everything ran smoothly. Helping out gave me a new appreciation for the work and the workers.

"Hey, Sean, you good with the audio setup?" A guy called Mike calls from across the sand, his hands full of coiled cables.

"Think so. Let's give it a try," I yell back.

I plug in a microphone and tap it a few times. My voice booms across the beach: "Check, check. One, two. Surfers, are you ready?"

A handful of early-bird competitors cheer in response. Looks like we're all set on that front. Then, Miles gathered everyone for a final team meeting. He stands on one of the lifeguard chairs, her face flushed with pride and exhaustion.

"I can't even begin to say how amazed I am by every single one of you. We had five days to do what seemed impossible, and yet, here we are. Mayor Bailey got the call confirming the water was clean and safe, and the stage was set. The surf is calling.

Tomorrow is Opening Day, and let's make it one nobody will ever forget!"

Cheers erupt, drowning out the sound of crashing waves. People high-five and hug, and even a few tears are shed. The sense of accomplishment is palpable; it buzzes in the air like electricity.

As I take a moment to soak it all in, Henry comes over, slapping me on the back. "We did it, dude. Against all odds, we did it."

"Yeah, we did," I agree, looking around at the beach — our beach —where, for a few days, the surf community and townspeople came together to celebrate the sport we love.

I took a seat in the shade and sipped a frozen lemonade. The town was ready for the influx of surfers and tourists, but if the way I felt was anything to go by, everyone who'd been responsible for making it so was bone tired. The lemonade gave me a brain freeze, and it was minutes before I realized my phone was buzzing. I pulled it out of the deep side pocket of my cargo shorts. It was a text from Lizzie.

See you in 30.

I exhaled a deep breath. I wasn't sure what condition the house was in, considering Drew, Will, Art, and I hadn't done much housework since hunkering down from the storm, but I was pretty sure it could stand some picking up and airing out. I hurried to my truck, hopped in and headed home. Hopefully, the boys were home. They could help me straighten up.

No one was home, but it wasn't too bad. I opened the doors

and windows, let in the fresh, perfumed air of the garden, and tidied up. When my family arrived, I swung the door wide and stepped out on the porch to greet them. My mother, sister, and two young nephews spilled out of the big Rover, hauling suitcases, bags of groceries, and who-knew-what-else. I jogged down the steps to the driveway to help them bring everything inside.

"Uncle Sean!" Sammy and George ran up to me, nearly tackling me to the ground with their enthusiastic hugs. They were buzzing with youthful energy, faces flushed from the excitement.

"Hey, you rascals!" I managed to say, putting fourteen-year-old Sammy into a headlock and squeezing him against my side. "You guys ready to have some fun?"

George jumped up, grabbed my other arm, and hung from it like it was a tree branch. "Yeah!" he shouted, his eyes wide with joy and anticipation.

Mum and Lizzie approached, each pulling rolling luggage and carrying big purses. There were more bags of groceries, blankets, pillows and who knew what, at the foot of the steps.

"Stop attacking your uncle and help bring those things in," Lizzie told her boys, tipping her head towards the front door. The boys went down the stairs to grab whatever they could carry, and I followed them to bring in the groceries.

"Ma, Lizzie, you moving in or what?" I asked jokingly, holding four bags of unwieldy groceries.

"You wish," Mum said, hugging me tightly. "We just came prepared."

"Prepared for what? We have grocery stores, you know."

Lizzie rolled her eyes. "Mum brought half the kitchen, and I couldn't talk her out of it."

"Who knew what the shelves in the stores looked like after a cyclone. They could've been empty, then what?"

"Then we would've gone out to eat. But thank you, Mum. I love your cooking." I gave her a kiss on the cheek and took the bags to the kitchen.

Before long, Mum and Lizzie had taken over the kitchen, making everything sparkle like it had when it was brand new and then filling the house with the aromas of home-cooked meals. The blender whirred, the oven beeped, and the chatter was endless. Meanwhile, Sammy and George, armed with toy swords, declared the living room their "pirate territory."

Amidst the chaos, Drew and his friends came home and stopped in their tracks. "What's happening, Uncle Sean? You have company?"

"Sort of," I said, grinning. "Come see."

Drew's eyes widened when he saw Mum and Lizzie. "Whoa, Mum. Grandma. You're here."

"Apparently," Lizzie said, wiping her hands on a towel tucked into her apron and coming over to hug her son. "Not that you invited us to come see you surf in this *Wave* Competition."

"I…I was going to call you after. To explain…"

"And we would have missed seeing you win for ourselves."

"Come give your grandma a hug, Drew," Mum said, holding out her hands. He did as she bid, and she pat him on the back. "I think you boys need proper nourishment before this big competition. Need good food to keep your stamina."

"Hello Arthur, William. I'm Drew's mother, Elizabeth. This is my mother, Charlotte Hargrove," Lizzie said to Drew's friends, who were still standing near the door. "Are you boys hungry?"

"Yes, Ma'am," they said in unison.

"Well, get cleaned up. Dinner will be ready shortly.

My Mother took off her apron, folded it and put it away, then sat on a stool at the counter. "Sean, Drew, you two set the table. George, you take out the trash. It's piling up."

"Grandma, I don't know where the trash is," George whined, and Drew and I exchanged glances. When Mum and Lizzie told you to do something, even as old as I am, you didn't argue or balk; you just did as you were told. Except that didn't always include George. I think my mom loved him best. However, she gave him a pointed look, which I then intercepted. "I'll get the trash, Mum. Just let me show Drew where the good dishes are."

Dinner was a feast, and afterward, as the sun was starting to set, we went down to the beach. The boys decided to forgo their last set of practice drills, and with tomorrow being Opening Day, I figured if they were ready by now, they still had time to make a good showing next year. Drew brought his surfboard down and gave Sammy and George s few basic surf lessons. Their laughter and splashes filled the air, mingling with the cries of seagulls. Lizzie and Mum sat on camp chairs beneath giant beach umbrellas that I'd hauled down the rockface. As evening faded into night, we climbed the steps, sandy and exhausted but happy.

It was still pretty early for Drew, Art, Will, and I to turn in. Neither, apparently, were Sammy and George. All of the guys had congregated in the main room, and Will nudged me as he passed me in the kitchen. "Hey, Uncle, you up for some gaming? We're going to play video games."

I looked over at Drew, who was already setting up his gaming console, cords sprawling everywhere like spaghetti. Will and Art were grabbing their favorite game controllers, already deep in banter about who was going to be which character, and Sammy and George sat looking on.

"I'll watch. Maybe Sammy can play?"

As I settled into an armchair, George perched on the armrest next to me, and we watched on as Drew, Will, Art, and Sammy pushed and shoved each other on the sofa, their voices loud and animated, their eyes fixed on the TV screen. With the cacophony of sound effects, virtual explosions, shoutouts from the video game, and their raucous commentary, the noise was near deafening.

"No way! I totally had you!" Drew yelled, elbowing Art, then leaning forward as if trying to physically enter the game.

"Keep dreaming, both of you," Will retorted, his fingers flying over the controller buttons. "You can't handle this."

Art, usually the quiet one, surprised everyone by launching a virtual attack that wiped out both Drew and Will's characters. "Bow down to the underdog," he said, grinning broadly.

Meanwhile, Sammy, who had the least experience but the most enthusiasm, screamed from overstimulated male testosterone every time he managed to do anything. "I got someone! I got someone!" he yelled, his face a canvas of pure joy.

George leaned in and whispered, "You know, this is more intense than sports matches."

"I know, right?" I agreed. "It's like watching gladiators, just with less blood and more trash talk."

As the game reached its climax, tensions ran high. Drew, Will, and Art were neck and neck, their characters circling each other in a virtual standoff. Sammy, bless his heart, had somehow managed to stay in the game, his character hiding behind virtual obstacles.

"Three... two... one...," counted down the game, and then all hell broke loose. There was screaming and yelling, and finally, the screen displayed in big, bold letters: GAME OVER.

And the winner was—Art. He threw his arms up in victory, a triumphant smile on his face.

"I demand a rematch!" Drew huffed, clearly not used to losing.

"Yeah, me too," Will seconded, "but maybe after some sleep."

George looked at me, both of us sharing a silent moment of amusement. "Well, that was... intense."

"Yes, indeed," I said. "But you know what? It's these crazy, intense, utterly ridiculous family moments that make everything worthwhile."

George nodded, his eyes filled with a mix of exhaustion and contentment. "Yeah, they do."

The boys began to disperse, retreating to their rooms in a post-gaming haze; the house settled into a quieter rhythm.

"Lord, what a mess," Mum said, but her eyes twinkled with delight. "It's like a tornado hit this place."

"Only a tornado of testosterone and video game rage," Lizzie added, grabbing a few empty soda cans and dumping them into a trash bag.

"Go on to bed, Guys. I've got this," I said, picking up the controllers and started wrapping up the cords. "I know you're tired. It won't take me long."

"Well, they can help, and it'll go even that much faster," Lizzie interjected. Sheepishly, the five boys began to pick up their mess. No one was willing to gainsay her.

My mum paused, holding a half-empty bowl of popcorn in her hands. "You're looking much better, Sean. You were so worn out when you got back from America in October. It worried me."

Lizzie nodded, tying up the trash bag with more force than necessary. "Yeah, we were really concerned, especially with you leaving again so soon."

I sighed, remembering that difficult time. I'd returned from the States exhausted, not just physically but emotionally.

"I was a mess, wasn't I? But it feels like I've hit the reset button. I've come back to life."

Mum put down the popcorn bowl and came over to hug me. "That's good."

"Why did you buy this house, though," Lizzie asked, taking a seat on the armrest of the couch, her cleaning task momentarily forgotten. "And you renovated it from the ground up? I mean, it's beautiful and all, but …why?"

"It was an impulse purchase. I saw it, and I wanted it. I dunno, I thought maybe we could use it for holidays away from the city," I said, taking a deep breath.

"Well, it certainly is a ways away from the city."

"Will you come up here for vacations?"

"Yeah, I think it'll be good to get out of the city. We would benefit from having a place by the beach where we can have a nice holiday whenever we can all get away."

"I was hoping so. It really was a great deal, and I couldn't pass it up. I'm glad you like it."

Lizzie got up, stretching her arms over her head. "I'm bushed, guys. I think we can leave the rest until tomorrow. I'll get up early and come clean everything up."

I looked around. It really wasn't that much more to do, and I would get it all up once they went to their room. Today had been a long and busy day for all of us, and after nearly a week with barely any sleep, it was also taking its toll on me. I gave them a hug and a peck on the forehead and shooed them into the main floor guest room. It didn't take me long to straighten up, and as I headed to my rooms upstairs, I felt a profound sense of peace wash over me. Lying in bed, enveloped in pitch darkness, I remembered how I felt on the plane coming home from San Diego and those weeks in the condo compared to how I felt now. Even I could see how far I'd come in the last couple of months. From the depths of depression to this—a house filled with my family and laughter, arguments, messes, and most importantly, unconditional love. In that quiet moment before sleep claimed me, I smiled and huffed, unable to get out a full chuckle. I was so grateful… for everything.

~

On Opening Day, the competition area on the beach is bustling with energy that drowns out the sound of crashing waves in the distance. The guys have been up since the crack of dawn, waxing their boards and checking—and rechecking—their gear. As we go to the check-in tent, I see them looking around anxiously, trying to keep their nerves under wraps. I step to the side, letting them approach the registration desk and scan the organized chaos around us. My God, it felt like yesterday when it was me doing this.

"Name?" the volunteer at the desk asks without looking up, and I hear him say. "Drew, Drew Portman." I smiled. He sounded twelve years old.

"Ah, yes. You're in Heat number three. Here's your jersey." She hands him a bright yellow jersey, which he clutches like it's some kind of sacred artifact. "The briefing will start in about twenty minutes."

"Thanks."

We wait for Art and Will to get registered and receive their jerseys before heading toward the designated area where the competitors can leave their gear. It's a sea of surfboards, like a forest of fiberglass and foam. They find a spot, place their boards carefully on the rack, and pull on their shirts.

Bight. Colorful surfboards were lined up, gleaming in the early morning light like rows of candy-colored missiles. The atmosphere was electric. Everyone was buzzing, riding on pure nerves and sheer excitement.

"So, are you ready to take the plunge, man?" Will asks, nudging Art with an elbow.

"Born ready," he said, grinning from ear to ear.

"Riders meeting in five!" calls out the announcer from the stage. I left them to follow the flow of competitors as they gathered and headed to the competitor's area.

"Alright, everyone, I want to welcome you to the Opening Day of the Big Wave Amateur Surf Challenge! Thanks to Mother Nature for giving us a break with that storm, eh?" shouted a man, likely an event exec, booming into the mic, which blared out over the speakers. There was a collective cheer, and he continued. "Today, we'll kick off the first set of heats. Five riders per heat; the top two move on. We have a lot of ground to cover, so let's keep this crisp."

Drew, Will and Art leave, entering the area cordoned off for the competitors, and I decide to check out the arcades and food vendors. The town is like a carnival, and I don't know which way to go first. Food trucks are lined up bumper to bumper in the parking lot close to the beach, and the smell of saltwater and sunscreen mixed with the odor of oil searing on the hot grills and meat, fish and veggies frying up is almost overwhelming. Further back from the beach are food booths with picnic tables set in a grassy, shaded area. Each vendor offers a different culinary experience. I hurry past them, taking shallow breaths of the mix of aromas. I smell fresh tacos, the handmade tortillas sizzling on the grill, and the toppings a rainbow of fresh veggies and salsas. Next door to that is an Asian fusion booth that served up steaming bao buns and skewers of grilled meats that were hissing and popping over hot coals. A few steps away, the heady aroma of garlic and basil wafts from a booth specializing in gourmet flatbreads, their thin crusts bubbling up in a wood-fired oven.

Naturally, there's the grill joint, where you can almost hear the low-and-slow cooked meats sizzling and barbeque sauces in shades from molasses-dark to pepper-red in covered bowls, just waiting to be slather on a pulled pork or beef brisket sandwich. At the end of the triple rows of food stalls with a wide enough thoroughfare in between them is a shop that's like a Willy Wonka fantasy, with towers of rainbow macarons and delicate pastries. The one beside it specializes in exotic ice creams, with flavors like lavender honey and matcha-coconut that I wasn't sure I wanted to try.

It is amazing to see so many trucks, booths or vendors here. We were still trying to pick up behind Cyclone Leslie less than twenty-four hours ago, feeling grateful that there'd been minimal damage to the area. I keep walking, and soon, a wave of sound hits me—laughter, chatter, music. I'd found the game arcades. They were set up a good distance from the competition, and I could barely hear the announcer making calls on the beach. Bright flags and banners flapped in the wind, each one carrying the logo of the event or a sponsor. I crossed the road and stepped onto a smaller boardwalk set up just for the vendor booths selling surf gear, local crafts, and all kinds of memorabilia. Even here, it was busy. People were busy snapping selfies in front of larger-than-life sand sculptures and posing in front of colorful murals or with prop surfboards. Everywhere I looked, there were colors—wetsuits in neon hues, surfboards with psychedelic patterns, and even the crowd seemed to have coordinated, wearing the event's official merch or just rocking some serious beach style.

Finally, I saw what I was looking for. Stepping inside a giant tent where the games were set up was like stepping into another dimension. The booths were lit by a kaleidoscope of neon lights, casting colorful glows on the plank floors. Retro and modern collide here; vintage pinball machines line one wall, their analog dings and clinks a soothing nostalgia. Right next to them, state-of-the-art virtual reality stations invite you into futuristic landscapes. Classic video game machines formed a labyrinth in the center of the floor, rapid-fire clicking of joystick battles and the unmistakable sounds of old-school favorites—including 'Pac-Man' gobbling up pellets and the pew-pew of 'Space Invaders.' Adjacent to them, racing simulators offer bucket seats and steering wheels, where gamers could take on winding roads at breakneck speeds, their faces lit up by the high-res screens. Over in a brightly lit corner, skeeball lanes have people rolling for high scores and glory, and claw machines temped patrons with their plushie prizes as they passed on their way to and from a lounge area.

Wandering through this maze of lights and sounds, I felt a pang of envy at the simple joys and carefree laughter around me. I hadn't been to an arcade-like this or walked around a town while a surfing event was being held in more than a decade, maybe even longer. As a competitor on the circuit, we'd fly in, stay close to the beach and the competition, and fly out. There was no time to walk around to enjoy whatever the town had to offer. With a deep breath, I took one last look at this other world, then left the grounds, heading back toward the beach. The competition had already started, and I hurried to find a good spot to size up the competition. Cal would be hard to beat, but I wanted to see who else might be strong competition for Drew, Art, and Will.

CHAPTER
FIFTEEN

As expected, Cal turned in a spectacular performance and immediately shot to the top of the rankings.

Many of the young competitors shook their heads, knowing they were going to have to go above and beyond anything they'd ever done to catch him, much less beat him. The horn sounded over my head, and I instinctively ducked. It signaled the start of Drew's heat, and I watched as he entered the water and paddled out to the lineup. I pulled out my new binoculars to focus on his bright yellow jersey. I saw him sit for a moment, even as others took off after several rolling waves, then he zeroed in on the one he wanted and paddled like mad, his arms propelling him forward. I saw the wave lift him, and he popped up swiftly. I can't hear myself, but I know I am yelling and screaming with the crowd as he rides the wave, carving a path along its face.

As the wave started to close out, I watched him kick out and start paddling back. It was a good ride, but the heat wasn't over yet. He has two more waves, two more chances to prove himself. The minutes ticked by, each one stretching longer than the last as I watched his every move. Finally, the horn sounded again, and the heat was over. I took a deep breath, one I didn't know I'd been holding and waited for him to come ashore. The scores would be up soon, but right now, at this moment, I felt like he'd already won. As he hit the beach, he looked for me, and when he saw me, a grin stretched across his face.

"Dude, that was sick!" he says, and we share a high-five that stings my palm in the best way possible.

"Yeah, man, you killed it," I reply, though the official results are still to come. But that didn't matter right then. What mattered was sharing Drew's happiness and the indescribable blend of exhaustion and elation I knew he was experiencing. We walked over to where Lizzie, Mum, George and Sammy were sitting so he could sit and catch his breath. I left him there as Art and Will were up next, and I wanted to see their heat.

The next morning, the lads had to get signed in and gather in the competitors' area by 7:15. They got up at five with me, ate a very light breakfast, and left the house in plenty of time. I hung around, helping Lizzie pack hampers of food and drinks to carry down to the beach. We also hauled down camping chairs. Tent sails and poles on which to secure them, blankets and towels, a big satchel with everything else but the kitchen sink.

Once they were settled and the men's division heats had started, I bounced back and forth, watching the heats from the waterline and checking on my family further up the sandy beach. Several times, I saw surfers hanging around, eating sandwiches and slices of pie, and sipping cups of icy lemonade while regaling Mum and Lizzie with stories of their surfing exploits. I'd made sure to spoil their fun by plopping down in the middle of the blanket and glaring at the intruders. The men got the message after a few minutes and slipped away. Lizzie swiped at me with a beach towel, laughing at my obvious intentions, and I'd run back to the waterline to watch whichever of my boys' turn it was to compete.

Around eleven, the announcer called the midday break, and we packed everything up and took it back to the house where Drew, Will and Art rested and ate. I left them sprawled on the sofa, and Mum and Lizzie put the food away. I pulled a baseball cap down low and slid on a pair of sunglasses, having decided to take a walk among the multitude. I thought I looked enough like a regular guy, able to blend in with the crowd, but there were so many fans in town that many of them recognized me instantly. So many people stopped me, asking for autographs, snapshots and selfies, that just walking from one area of the beach to another became a tactical maneuver. It wasn't that I didn't appreciate the enthusiasm or the fans—it was just that I didn't want to be a part of the celebrity frenzy. There were quite a few big-name surfers around, ready to rub elbows with the young up-and-comers and participate as guest judges and commentators.

I crossed the sand and took the main thoroughfare that led up from the beach and intersected with High Street. Twice, I ducked a group of enthusiastic fans who looked like they were on a mission, but eventually, I was spotted by a young kid who caught me out, his eyes wide with recognition. I stopped for him. I couldn't be rude. He was such a cute kid and exceedingly polite.

"You're Sean Hargrove, right?" When I nodded, he gave a whoop of enthusiasm. "You're a legend? My Dad and I have been following your career for years!" I chuckled, ruffling his hair. I don't know how many years he'd been following me, considering he had to be nine or ten at the most, but I yielded when he asked me to autograph his souvenir book and take a selfie. I chuckled and waved his father over to get in the picture with us.

After that, I put my head down and kept walking—past the bakery, where people had started queuing up outside, past the bookshop and other stores along High Street, and past Lily's, which also had a line of people waiting outside. I was somewhat surprised that the restaurants were queuing up with so many food trucks and booths along the beach.

I wasn't paying attention as I crossed the street, and I nearly bowled Lara over. She grabbed my arm to help her stay on her feet and laughed at my startled expression. "Lara. I'm so sorry."

"I was going to call you, but it seems we're attempting to be incognito," she teased.

I laughed, shrugging. "I'm not usually hanging out like this during competitions."

"You were the one competing. None of this mattered," she said, waving her hands around us.

"Yeah. I kinda like not being in the spotlight."

"Humph," she snorted as if that was hard to believe and looped her arm around mine. "Which way are you headed?"

"Thinking of going back home. I've been wandering around, getting some fresh air, but I think I've wasted enough time this morning. My Mum, sister and her kids are at the house with the nephews. Where are you off to?"

"To Lily's. The Inn is full, and the dining room is overflowing, and I'm on my way to see if she needs any help."

"You're a good grandchild," I said, patting her hand on my arm. "Tell Lily 'Hullo' for me."

"Will do. See you later." She turned me loose and ran across the street. I continued down the street, heading back towards the house.

The competition started up again in the evening as the temperatures began to moderate. I left Mum, Lizzie, Sammy, and George sitting on the beach in the camp chairs, with a couple of lit tiki torches behind them to keep the mosquitoes and other flying insects away. Certain they were comfortable and could see well enough, I left to find Drew.

"Uncle Sean!" I recognized his voice immediately and looked around, spotting him jogging across the sand. His face was practically glowing, and his eyes were round with excitement. "You won't believe what just happened!"

I raised an eyebrow, intrigued. "Alright, spill it. What's got you so worked up?"

He took a deep breath, trying to contain his enthusiasm, but it bubbled up regardless. "A guy came up to me. Said he's a management agent and wants me to give him a call after the competition. He says he's been watching me surf!" I felt a rush of pride for Drew but also a pang of protectiveness. "Really? Did he give you his name?"

"Yeah, he gave me his card. Here," he said, handing me a sleek black card with the name Alec R. Townsend embossed in gold. There were several logos of different renowned surf brands stamped below his contact details.

I smiled, "I think I've seen him around. I saw him watching Cal as well."

Drew's eyes lit up even more if that was possible. "He was watching Cal, too? So, he's legit then, right?"

I took a moment, observing Drew's hopeful expression. "It seems like it. But remember, it's always good to be cautious. What exactly did he say to you?" I was curious how Alec approached Drew. Did he know that Drew was his nephew, or if he'd seen something special in him?

Drew, catching on to my protective tone, tried to recall the conversation accurately. "He said he was impressed with my technique and style. Mentioned something about potential sponsorships and stuff. But to be honest, I was so excited, it's all become a bit of a blur now."

I placed a reassuring hand on Drew's shoulder. "This could be a great opportunity, but we need to approach it with our eyes wide open. We'll look into it; talk to him and maybe some other contacts I have. Right now, though, you've got to concentrate on doing a good job. Put the other stuff out of your head. This is what you've been training for."

Drew nodded, his initial excitement now tempered with a dose of reality. "Thanks. I just... it felt like a dream, you know?"

"I know." I smiled, giving him a one-armed hug. "I know exactly what you mean."

~

The evening men's division heats were killer, and practically whole teams of young hopefuls were being eliminated, one right after the other. Only one contender per team, unless there was a tie, could advance to the next level. I kept the running scores in my head, hoping none of my boys would be the next one to sit out. I was standing front and center when the horn signaled the end of the third round. Art shuffled out of the water, practically dragging his board. His usual energetic gait was slow and heavy, leaving deep footprints in the wet sand. He didn't look over at the cheering crowd or at me. His eyes were fixed on the ground, and his shoulders were slumped. I had to look away for a moment so he wouldn't catch me grinning.

"Dude, what's wrong?" I asked finally, tossing him a towel and following him over to our blankets. He shook his head and dropped his surfboard with a resigned thud rather than standing it up in the sand. When he sat down and looked at me, the downward curve of his lips spoke volumes. Mum leaned over and said something to him that I couldn't hear, and I saw his lips twitch. She must have said something to make him smile, at least a little.

"I'm out, Uncle Sean," he said to me.

"How do you know?"

"I know."

"Okay. Well, we'll talk about it later, okay." He nodded. "I'll be right back."

I sprinted back over to watch Will in the next heat. I staked out a spot at the waterline and used my binoculars to get a good look at him. He turned in a decent performance, enough to advance to the next round, as did Drew. Will made it through several more rounds before being eliminated. I can't say he was any less morose than Art had been, but his usual snarky demeanor was decidedly less so. He plopped down beside Art, his chest heaving dramatically, and their hunched-over silhouettes in the sand sun seemed to magnify their air of sadness. Again, my mother leaned over to say something, but because Will was sitting on the opposite side of Art, Art had to relay her message. Instantly, both boys were grinning. I watch the three of them, my eyes narrowed, and lips pursed.

"You guys okay over here?"

"We're fine, Hun," Mum answered without even looking over at me. Art and Will, however, did look up and nodded in agreement. I tipped my chin at them and turned around to go back and watch Drew.

Drew held on, scoring enough to advance to the finals the next morning. He was jubilant when he came over to sit down on the blankets.

"You guys okay?" he asked, knowing that both of his friends were finished in the competition.

"Yeah, I'm good," Art responded first. "But I can't believe I didn't last longer. Such a stupid mistake, and wham! It's all over."

"What actually happened?" Drew asked. I leaned forward just a little. I had seen everything, but I wanted to hear what Art had to say.

"I don't know. I thought I was good. I felt like I was in the zone, then the next thing I knew, I was in the drink. That cost me big time." We all felt bad for Art. I knew how hard he'd worked. Then, swiping his hand down his face, he looked up at us, grinning and said, "It wasn't funny until just now." And he burst into belly laughs. It was contagious, and we all fell apart. It really had been hilarious. I saw him when he flipped off his board and went down. When I saw it, I was like, "Wha…?" He splashed water on the entire group. I tried to stop laughing as Will started to speak.

"Yeah, the same with me," Will mumbled. He was the first to regain some semblance of composure. "I thought I had that wave."

He dug his fingers into the sand as if trying to grasp something solid and looked up at me, his eyes bright and sincere. "For real. I was ready for it. I thought I had anticipated what it was going to do next, but I guess I was way off."

I tried. I swear I tried, but I couldn't hold it. I doubled over, wailing with laughter. I think I set everyone off again. I saw it, and I'm sure Mum and Lizzie saw it as well. Will had been blindsided by that wave and rolled like a burrito. Ohmigod, my stomach was aching from laughing so hard that I just laid down, stretched out like I was about to make Angels in the sand.

"Anybody got a rabbit's foot or good luck piece?" Drew asked, coming up for air. "Not you guys, okay? We already know your good luck pieces don't work," he directed, pointing two fingers at his buddies. "I just don't want to go out like you two did." His voice wavered as he tried not to laugh again. Will and Art exchanged glances, sneered at their friend, and laid back on the blanket, their shared humiliation creating a deeper bond. Still grinning, I rolled over by Drew and laying on my stomach, I gave him a high five. We stayed together like that for a while until he punched me lightly in the shoulder, and I had to bring him down. Sammy and George piled on top of me, making me heavier and smashing Drew harder into the sand. Lizzie broke us up, swatting us with her towel.

"Get up. Get up, all of you. Can't take you nowhere."

CHAPTER
SIXTEEN

The day promised to be hot.

It was the last day of the heat wave and the last day of the competition. At the end of the heats last evening, the remaining contestants were told to assemble at six-thirty this morning. Art, Drew, and I came down with Drew to offer moral support. We watched him stand in line to sign in, his silhouette rimmed by the glow of the rising sun. I could feel the palpable energy of the beach, the electric buzz of anticipation in the air. A crowd had gathered, their chatter a constant hum, but my focus was solely on Drew. When he'd completed the sign-in, he walked down to the water's edge, eyes fixed on the horizon where the waves crashed with ferocious energy. His surfboard was wedged under his arm, fingers drumming on its smooth surface. I could see he was extremely nervous, possibly feeling a little sick in his stomach. He'd done this a hundred times before, yet today was different. The stakes were higher, the pressure immense.

"Drew!" I yelled, trying to get his attention. He glanced over, those bright eyes clouded with a mix of hope and anxiety. I beckoned him over, and he trudged through the sand, leaving a trail of deep footprints behind.

He stopped in front of me, wiping the sweat off his brow. "Uncle Sean," he began, voice quivering slightly, "I've never felt this nervous before. It's like my stomach's doing flips. I don't want to be sick."

I reached out, placing a comforting hand on his shoulder. "It's natural, kiddo. This is a big moment. But remember, you've trained hard for this. All those early mornings, the countless hours in the water... it's all led to this."

Drew nodded, taking a shaky breath. "I know, I know. It's just... second place. It's so close. I can almost taste it. But it's so tight. Everyone is a fraction of a point from everyone else."

I studied his face, noticing the faint lines of stress etching his youthful features. "Just promise me one thing," I began, my tone serious.

Drew raised an eyebrow, "Anything."

"Do your best and enjoy the ride. Win or lose, make it count."

He took a moment, letting my words sink in, then nodded with newfound resolve.

"And," I said, pulling him out of his thoughts, "No matter what happens out there, I'm proud of you. You've come so far and grown so much. Today is just another step in your journey."

He met my gaze, eyes glistening with unshed tears. "Thanks. That means the world to me."

I gave his shoulder one last squeeze. "Now, go out there and show them what you're made of. Ride those waves like you own them."

With renewed determination, Drew nodded, clutched his board, and headed back to the starting point. I watched him, heart swelling with pride and hope, silently cheering him on as he prepared to face the biggest challenge of his life.

Art and Will listened as I talked with Drew, standing outside the cordoned-off competitor area next to me.

"He has a real shot, doesn't he?"

"Yeah, Art, he does, but he's up against tough competition. You know. You were out there. But some of these guys have been surfing all their lives, every single day."

"Like that guy Cal. He's so far ahead, no one's likely to catch him," Will added.

"No, not likely. Drew is untested, just as you were. It's due to his indomitable will that he's made it this far."

Both Art and Will nodded, and we stood together, looking out at the ocean. Cal Eaton was in the first heat; Drew was in the third, and as Will had said, Cal would have to fall off his board every round to lose first place—maybe. He'd earned far more perfect tens and nine-point-this-or-that than anyone else in his heats, so it wasn't likely anyone was going to catch him, not even with a ten out of ten from Kenneth 'Kendo' McWhorter, another local boy, who was seeded to win second place. However, this final group of competitors was so tightly bunched that Kendo only held on by a short lead. There was a chance anyone could knock him out of it.

I saw Alec and Jim standing at the waterline not far from me, and I nodded at them. They were excited as Cal took to the water. The boy paddled out with five others, letting the water swell and roll beneath him. I followed him with my binoculars and watched him pop up when the wave surged. He came off the crest ever so smoothly and slid in through the back door of the massive cavern of a barrel. I knew what he was doing and feeling, as I had experienced it so many times. Being inside was timeless, the water blue and pristine, reflecting a light so white it hurt your eyes, and the noise was like the roar of supersonic jets. It was also a Zen moment when you couldn't resist the urge to reach out and touch the water as it cups and rolls over your head.

Cal emerged into bright sunshine, still perfectly balanced on his board, and the screams of the fans and announcers were ear-splitting. He blinked, as the bright sunshine was likely blinding, and let the tail end of the surge bring him in, breaking once it reached knee-deep water. Finally, he leaped off the board and threw his hands in the air, his head back, and screamed in jubilation. That had to be another perfect ten.

"Yes," I screamed, jumping up and down with the crowd.

I didn't even wait to see the following riders as I moved to intercept Cal as soon as he reached the beach. He swung his board up out of the water, clutching it tightly to his body with one hand, and slogged through the loose sand and receding water. Saltwater streamed down his face, stinging his eyes, finding its way into his open mouth, and dripping from his chin. He shook his head, flinging the water and hair off his face, and gave us a gleeful grin. Alec was first to reach him, tossing him a beach towel with PHARON Industries, a manufacturer of beachwear, printed down the middle. It was Cal's first endorsement.

"You did it, Dude, you did it," Alec shouted, "That was as perfect a ride as any I've ever seen. I approached them, Art and

Will behind me, and shook Cal's hand, a half-dozen colorful rubber bracelets hanging from his wrist, each a different neon color, and the familiar logo of Walter Industries, the manufacturer of the wetsuits I'd worn on the circuit, stamped clearly visible.

"You were awesome, Cal," Alec said. "I can't get over how good you looked out there. We have to thank Sean here for discovering you and letting us get the first peek at you. You're going to have every company in the industry ringing our phones from now on."

"And that's a good thing," I said, laughing but also totally serious. "Congratulations."

"Thank you, Mr. Hargrove. I appreciate everything you did."

"I made the phone calls. You did the rest. And keep in touch, okay? Let me know how this guy is treating you, yeah?"

"I will."

"Dude, take of yourself, okay?" Alec said, giving me a friendly jab to the shoulder. "Maybe we can get together when you get back to Sydney, "

"Sounds good. I'll give you a call when I get back." I turned to Jimmy, reaching over to shake his hand. "You're heading back to the States soon?"

"Yeah, catching the red-eye out tonight. I just wanted to be here to see Calvin win this challenge."

"Well, take care, my friend, and maybe we'll catch up when you come back to Sydney or the next time I'm in Florida."

"Looking forward to it. Alright, gentlemen, if you're ready…."

I stepped back and watched my friends walk away, their new protege between them. Art, Will, and Drew strolled over, their jaws practically unhinged.

"You know those guys? Aren't they scouts?"

"Yes, and I've known them for years. We worked the circuits together." I hooked my arm around Drew's neck, playfully squeezing it and ruffled his damp hair

"Did you just help Cal get discovered?" He asked, trying to walk beside me with his head clamped inside my armpit.

"My friends came down to see him for themselves. Calvin did the rest. Don't worry about it. When you're ready, your turn will come. Shouldn't you be heading down to the waterline, Drew? I think the horn's about to go off." I turned my nephew loose, and we followed him to the edge of the water.

I was probably as anxious, probably more than Drew. I positioned myself so I could watch his every move through my binoculars. At this point, they should have left bruised rings around my eyes. Then I saw Drew positioned himself, eyeing an approaching set. I sucked in my breath and held it as a wave began to form, then gathered momentum, its crest glistening under the sun. Drew paddled fiercely, aligning himself with its path, and just as it was about to break, he sprung to his feet, gracefully catching the wave's energy.

His ride was poetry in motion; his connection with the wave was evident in every twist, turn, and cutback. He carved downhill the wave's face, harnessing its power, then shot up to the lip, executing a flawless aerial before seamlessly re-entering the wave. As he rode the wave's shoulder, he transitioned into a series of rapid-fire maneuvers, displaying both technical prowess and artistic flair. The crowd erupted in cheers and applause. But it seemed Nature had had one last test for him, and I watched as the wave began to close out. It looked as though it would engulf Drew, yet, with impeccable timing, he pulled into the barrel, disappearing from view. Time seemed to stand still. My breath burned in my chest, and I let it out in an explosive burst and inhaled. And with a triumphant burst of speed, Drew emerged from the wave, riding his board smoothly towards the shore. The beach erupted in jubilation. That ride was nothing short of spectacular.

As Drew made his way back to the shore, the weight of his board seemed inconsequential compared to the gravity of what he'd just achieved. From my vantage point, I watched him, my heart swelling with a mix of pride and overwhelming emotion. Before he even reached dry land, I was on my feet, making my way to him. Drew, still catching his breath, looked up, and our eyes met. In that split second, words became superfluous. My eyes, gleaming with tears of pride, mirrored the joy and accomplishment in his.

"Drew," I began, my voice thick with emotion, "that was... incredible."

He laughed, a joyful, relieved sound. "Did you see that barrel? Thought I was a goner for a second there!"

I pulled him into a tight embrace, thumping his back. "You rode with your heart out there. And it showed. I couldn't be prouder.”

Breaking away, Drew looked around at the cheering crowd, the other competitors, and the vast ocean that had been both a challenge and an ally.

“Thanks, Uncle Sean. You know I couldn't have done it without you.”

I shook my head, placing a hand on his shoulder. “This was all you. The training, the guidance, it can only take you so far. Today, out there, it was all Drew. And you were magnificent.”

He grinned, wiping away saltwater – or perhaps they were tears. It was hard to tell. “Feels good. Really good.”

I smiled back, clapping him on the back.

“You've made us all proud. Not just for that ride, but for the heart, dedication, and passion you've shown throughout.”

Lizzie slowly approached us, her hands outstretched to grab Drew. Tears glistened in her eyes, her smile a mile wide.

“Oh, Drew,” she exclaimed, taking his face in her hands, “you were brilliant out there! Just brilliant!” She planted a firm kiss on his forehead. My mother grabbed him, even though he towered over her, and rocked him, a gesture so typically Mum, so full of love and pride. Sammy and George, ever the enthusiastic duo, rushed in, clapping Drew on the back and ruffling his salt-soaked hair. “Mate, that was unreal!” George spurted.

Sammy, nodding in agreement, added, “You owned that wave, Drew! Absolutely owned it!”

Art and Will, despite their own rollercoaster of emotions from the competition, were beaming with pride for their friend.

"Knew you had it in you," Art said, his voice tinged with admiration. Will punched Drew's arm lightly, chuckling, "Man, you set the bar high!"

Even among the broader crowd, some strangers came forward, nodding in acknowledgment of Drew's exceptional performance; their smiles and Shaka signs were a testament to the impact and perfection of his ride. As the group converged, there was a chorus of congratulations, claps, and cheerful banter. The energy was infectious, the shared joy palpable. Every hug, every pat on the back, and every cheer was a testament to Drew's achievement, but in the back of my mind, I think I was more ecstatic and relieved that it was over.

~

That evening, we gathered for the awards ceremony. The ocean had calmed, the waves now gentle whispers against the shore. But the atmosphere on the beach was far from serene. Competitors hugged and celebrated, some in triumph and others in consolation. The scoreboard, with its glaring numbers, stood tall and unforgiving. Drew had not finished in the top ten. Though he'd had some impressive rides off and on, his overall score had not been enough to make the cut.

My family and I sat apart from the crush of people crowding the speaker's platform, where the winners in all the divisions would receive their accolades, trophies, and awards. I was sitting in a camp chair beside Lizzie but got up to sit close to Drew on the blanket. The vibrant, hopeful boy from earlier seemed a world away. Now, he looked lost, shattered by the weight of dashed dreams.

"Drew," I began softly, hesitating as he didn't acknowledge my presence.

Minutes stretched on, feeling like hours. Finally, he looked at me, his voice barely above a whisper. "I was so close. I could feel it. The roar of the crowd, the rush of the wave; it felt like destiny."

I knelt beside him, the coarse sand digging into my knees. "I saw you out there. You were incredible. You rode with your heart, with passion."

He gave a bitter laugh, looking up with red, swollen eyes. "Passion doesn't win challenges. Scores do. And mine... weren't good enough."

I took a deep breath, searching for the right words. "Life, Drew. It's all unpredictable. A random toss of the dice. We can give our absolute best, pour our soul into something, and still not get the outcome we desire. But that doesn't diminish your effort or worth."

His shoulders slumped. "I just... I wanted to make you proud. To show everyone that I belonged among the best."

I reached out, cupping his shoulder gently. "You did make me proud. More than you'll ever know. Not because of a rank or a score but because you gave it your all. You faced your fears, challenged the odds, and showed immense character. That's what truly matters."

He leaned into my touch, his eyes glistening with unshed tears. "It just hurts so much."

"I know, kiddo. I know. But remember, every setback is a lesson. It's what we take from it, how we grow and move forward, that defines us. This doesn't have to be the end. It can be the beginning."

"You're right, of course. I'm acting like a kid."

"It's okay. And there's always next summer break." He smiled with only one side of his lips raised, resigned to his promise that he would go back to school if this hadn't worked out according to his plans.

"The Big Wave Challenge will be back next year. So will I."

"And so will I."

This time, he chuckled. We sat together on the blanket and watched the ceremony, happy for those who had made it to the winner's circle.

CHAPTER SEVENTEEN

The town of Carmichael was slowly returning to normal, a quaint and sleepy village, now that the Surf Challenge was over and most of the tourists had left.

Residents were busy removing the temporary structures along the beach, and signs and banners were being removed from the lamp posts and store windows. My family was leaving today as well. Lizzie had to be back at work on Monday, and classes awaited for Drew and his friends. We'd enjoyed a few days of quiet and relaxation together after the competition ended, and I'd been happy to have them around me.

Mum and Lizzie, Sammy and George were downstairs in the two guest rooms on the main floor gathering their belongings and packing them in the back of the Rover, and Drew, Art and Will were upstairs in the two guest rooms next to me doing the same. I left out of my bedroom and knocked on Drew's door to see how he was coming. Music was filling the room from the little speaker connected to his mobile phone, and his belongings were spread out on the bed, the floor and every other surface in the room — his surf gear, clothes, books, and souvenirs of the summer. I looked on with a mix of melancholy and happiness. I leaned against the doorframe, watching him organize everything into multiple duffle bags.

"You know," I began, my voice gentle, "I'm proud of you. Not just for giving the competition your all, but for keeping your promise."

Drew paused, a shirt in his hand. He looked up, a hint of curiosity in his eyes. "Which promise?"

"The one about returning to the university," I replied with a knowing smile. "It's not easy to juggle your passion and your studies, but at least you're trying to strike a balance."

Drew chuckled, resuming his packing. "Yeah, well, I've always been a bit of a nerd. Besides, I made a commitment to myself and to you. And like you said, there's always next summer."

I walked over and sat on a chair, taking up the yellow jersey he'd worn in the challenge. "You know, it's not just about the competition. It's about growth, learning, and evolving. The university will offer you experiences and knowledge that will shape you in ways you can't even imagine."

Drew nodded, a thoughtful expression on his face. "I'm actually kind of excited to go back. I actually like my classes and… hanging out with some of the girls on campus. I didn't get to hang out once while we were here."

I laughed. "That's my boy!"

Drew grinned, punching me lightly in the arm. "Thanks. For everything. This summer's really been great."

"Next year." I pointed at him and left the room, feeling very proud of him. I headed next door and rapped on the open door of Art and Will's room.

"Morning, Uncle," Art greeted, his voice tinged with laughter.

"Good morning, Uncle," Will also responded.

"How are you two coming. I thought Sammy and George had switched rooms with you guys; so much noise coming out of here."

"We're good. Feels weird that summer's over, and we're packing up, heading back to the grind." Will said, balling up the shirts on his bed and tossing them into his duffle bag along with everything else.

"It's been quite the summer, hasn't it? Feels like just yesterday, you three rolling up with dreams of conquering the waves."

Art chuckled, "Yeah, and conquer we did! Well, at least we tried."

Will nudged him playfully, "Speak for yourself! I had that one epic ride. Almost felt like a pro!"

I laughed, unsure which ride Will believed had been epic but happy they'd enjoyed the summer. "You both did great. More importantly, you learned and grew. Not just as surfers, but as young men."

There was a moment of silence, the gravity of my remark settling on them. They had changed, and it was very apparent to me.

"You know, staying here, training with you has been so cool, you know? You made us feel like family. We came as friends, but now... we're family."

Will nodded. "Staying here has been awesome. This house

is like the coolest getaway. I'll remember this summer forever."

I felt a lump in my throat, touched by their words. "You boys are always welcome here. Remember that. And as for the university, tackle it with the same passion and determination you showed here. You'll ace it."

Will grinned, "We've made a pact. School first, then back to the waves. Next summer, we're coming back stronger."

Art added, "And with you helping us, we're unstoppable."

I gave them both high-fives, feeling the bond that had formed over the summer. "The waves will be waiting, and so will I." They promised, and I left them to finish up.

I went downstairs, where Mum and Lizzie were packing and tidying up. There was a fresh pot of coffee in the kitchen, and I went in to get myself a cup. I was humming a song in my head as I reached into the cabinet for a mug, and I didn't hear Mum come in behind me. I turned to see her climbing up on a stool at the island, her beautiful brown eyes practically staring through me. Her expression was one of years of love and wisdom.

"Son," she began, her voice soft, "I wanted to have a word with you before we head back."

I nodded, got my coffee and went around the island to sit on a stool next to her. She turned to me, her gaze searching mine.

"I know you've been struggling, carrying the weight of that day. The guilt, the pain... I was glad you came home. It's taken a heavy toll on you. But you look really good now. Happy and relaxed. Peaceful almost."

"I don't know if I'm at peace with everything," I answer,

"but I do feel better. It was hard. I survived. Colin didn't, and that was not my fault. Josh… his career, his dreams were shattered, but that wasn't my fault either. The damn shark wasn't my fault. I can say that now. None of it was my fault. Nothing that happened was anything that I could have changed. I know it. I can say it now. I wish…I wish I could have done more."

Mum's eyes met mine, a deep and soulful connection opening between us. I notice the lines on her face, the years of worry etched there, and I feel a twinge of guilt.

"It's taken a heavy toll on you, too," I said softly, my voice tinged with regret. "

She nods, likely feeling the weight of my words, sensing the release they bring me. Reaching out, she cups my face with both hands, forcing me to meet her gaze. "Life is fickle, my love. You know we don't get to choose the cards we're dealt. But it's up to us how we play them."

I swallowed hard, the lump in my throat growing. "I know, Mum. When I first came here, I needed to think, to find my purpose…."

"You came up here because you were running away. You were trying to avoid your demons." Mum's eyes filled with tears, but her voice remained steady. "I've watched you, Sean, support Colin and Josh, and now Drew, Art, and Will. I've watched you give everyone the best part of you. I saw you. You did good, but that was just the beginning. A good beginning, but a beginning, nonetheless. Promise me you'll come home and get some help. Speak to someone, a professional. Don't let the past steal your future. Josh has lost much, but he is trying to move past it. If he can, you can."

I nodded. "I promise, I'll try."

"Not try. Do." She kissed my forehead, her touch filled with love and concern. "You're not alone. You have us, your family. We will help you if you let us. You're such a private, prickly person, but we're here for you, and we'll get through this together."

As we sat there, wrapped in a comforting silence, I felt a glimmer of hope. Mum was right. I was good at giving all kinds of good advice, and these young'uns were good about heeding it. Now, I needed to do the same for myself. No one blamed me for Colin's death and Josh's devastating injuries. I did it to myself. I blamed myself. I'd made it all about me. I couldn't save them. It was my fault that I hadn't seen the shark in time. Why couldn't I have reached Colin before he disappeared beneath the waves? Why was I so far out, away from my friends?

Yeah, Mum was probably right. I had been running from a guilt that I heaped upon myself. It made me sound narcissistic, and I really wasn't that kind of guy.

I felt Mum getting down off the stool beside me, and I took her hand and gave it a squeeze.

"I'll be home in a couple of weeks."

"Come by when you get in."

"I will. I love you, Mum."

"I know, and I love you more."

It was nearly noon by the time everyone was in their respective vehicles, ready to make the drive back home and back to school. I'd said goodbye to Drew, Art and Will while they'd packed up their truck, but they couldn't leave until my sister pulled off, her Rover blocking them in. I approached Lizzie as she was about to climb into her vehicle, enveloping her in a hug. She hugged me back, her embrace warm and full of affection.

"You guys have everything?" I asked.

"I hope so. But if we've forgotten anything, bring it home with you."

"I will."

"You take care, little brother," she whispered, her voice tinged with emotion, and I squeezed her tight.

"Always, Sis. Always."

Mum stood nearby, her eyes already glistening with impending tears. I went to her, wrapping her in a tender embrace.

"I'm so proud of you, Sean," she murmured, "and we're so grateful for everything you've done for Drew, for the whole family, really."

I kissed her forehead, a gesture of deep love and respect. "It's been a journey, Mum. And having all of you here made it even more special."

A sudden, playful shove from the side broke the moment. Sammy, with his trademark grin, challenged me.

"Think you can still take me, Uncle Sean?"

I laughed, effortlessly lifting him off the ground in a playful wrestle, both of us laughing heartily. After a moment, I set him down, ruffling his hair, saying,

"Give it a few more years, champ! I want you to look after

your Mother and Grandmother. You're in charge, Okay?"

"You got it. I'm in charge."

"Don't go putting crazy ideas in his head, Sean," Lizzie yelled from inside the car. George, with his round glasses and dark, tousled hair reminiscent of a famous young wizard, looked up at me with wide eyes and admiration.

"Will you teach me to surf next time, Uncle Sean?" I knelt down, bringing myself to eye level with him. "Absolutely," I solemnly promised. "Next summer, it's you and me against the waves." He jumped and gave a loud whoop.

They were all in their cars and ready to go. I patted the side of the Rover and stepped back out of the way. The engine roared to life, and she honked her horn. Her car began to pull out of the driveway, and the boy's truck followed with Will behind the wheel. I watched them roll down to the main road, smiling and waving goodbye. I stood there until my entire family slowly disappeared down the road.

~

It was time for me to leave Carmichael. I'd spent another few days after my family left getting the house cleaned up and cleaned out. Lily had come over with several young housekeepers who worked in her Inn to oversee getting the place spic-and-span, and Henry Hayes promised to come out the next day with a few workers to board it up for the year. I didn't think I'd be back before next summer.

It was a beautiful day. Mother Nature must have gotten the memo that it was autumn. My truck was packed to bursting, and I was ready to pull out, but I had one more stop, this time at the diner. I parked in front of the glass-paned, double doors of Lily's Cafe and Inn, and the scent of fresh coffee and pastries filled the air as I walked inside. The familiar chime above the entrance announced my presence, and I scanned the room, looking for her familiar face. Behind the front desk, amidst an array of reservations and ledgers, stood Lily. Her eyes lit up upon seeing me, and she immediately set aside the paperwork, greeting me with that warm, inviting smile I had grown so fond of.

"Sean," she exclaimed, coming out from behind the desk to give me a hug.

"Lily," I responded, my voice betraying a hint of sadness. She could always read me, even without words. She enveloped me in a comforting hug, her gesture filled with the genuine affection built over our time of friendship.

"I hate to see you leave." She murmured, her voice slightly muffled against my shoulder. Pulling back, she fixed me with a stern yet playful look. "You better not become a stranger! I expect you to visit, especially during next year's contest."

I chuckled, appreciating her straightforwardness. "I promise. This place... and your fantastic coffee have left quite the impression."

She laughed, "It's not just the coffee, and you know it."

Feeling a surge of gratitude, I reached into my pocket, handing her a small card. "My mobile number. We've become such good friends, and I don't intend to lose that just because of distance. Call me anytime."

Lily took the card, her eyes misting over slightly. "Thank you, Sean. And remember, you always have a home here, even if it's just for a cup of coffee and some chatter."

I nodded, holding back my own emotions.

"Well, that's good to hear. While they're finishing up your order in the kitchen, you have time to say goodbye to Lara. She's in her office." she said conspiratorially.

"Thanks." I stepped around the front desk and walked down the corridor towards the back of the building. The muted, golden light from the morning sun streamed through the tall windows on the back wall, casting long streamers of light on the well-worn runners on the floor and the faded paintings hanging on the corridor walls.

Lara's office was located at the end of a corridor, its door slightly ajar. I could hear the gentle scratch of a pen on paper. Pushing the door open, I stepped into a room that was a mirror of Lara's personality – elegant, warm, and filled with little memories. Photos adorned the walls, and bookshelves brimmed with novels and journals. In the midst of it all, Lara sat at an antique desk, lost in her paperwork. She looked up, surprise registering in her beautiful eyes, followed quickly by a rush of emotion.

"Sean," she breathed, a subtle quiver in her voice.

"Hey, Lara," I said softly, my gaze taking in the details of her face, the hint of sadness in her eyes. "I couldn't leave without saying goodbye."

She set her pen down, clasping her hands in front of her. "Part of me hoped you would come by, but another part... wasn't so sure."

The distance between us felt as big as a chasm, full of tangled emotions, difficult-to-form words, and missed opportunities.

"You know," I began, keeping the heaviness I felt out of my voice, "we had great moments, fun ones, and I admit, I thought we might have something real, but...I'm glad we're still friends. Friends mean a lot to me."

Lara nodded slowly, her eyes moistening. "I felt it too, Sean. But I couldn't...."

"I know." Walking over, I leaned against the edge of her desk, searching her face for understanding. "It's not about fault or blame, Lara. Some connections are like a slow burn, growing over time. And others, they're like wildfires, consuming everything instantly. There's still time for us. Just not right now."

She looked up, her lips curving into a bittersweet smile. "Caught in the in-between. That's rather poetic in its own way, don't you think?"

Reaching out, I took her hand, feeling its warmth, its familiarity. "I truly cherished our time together, but in the meantime, our friendship thrives."

She squeezed my hand, tears slowly spilling over, making her bright blue eyes glisten. Her smile was the brightest I'd ever seen. I gently pulled her into an embrace, both of us finding solace in the warmth of the moment. As we parted, I cupped her face, brushing away her tears with my thumb before placing a tender kiss on her forehead.

"À plus tard, Sean," Lara whispered, and I stepped back, grinning.

"I thought you didn't know any French."

"I've been practicing how to say goodbye without saying Goodbye."

"À plus tard, Lara." I dropped my arms and turned around, and without looking back, I walked out of the room, pulling the door behind me and closing it with a soft click.

My order was ready when I returned to the lobby, a large cardboard box with fresh lunch and dinner entrees, fruit, sweet pastries, and a whole German Chocolate cake waiting for me. German Chocolate was Charlie's favorite. I put the box on the front seat of the truck, fixing the seat so that it wedges the box up against the dashboard. I didn't want it shifting while I drove. I started the engine, its soft hum merging with the distant sound of waves. With one last lingering look, I pulled out of the town square and headed towards M1. Once on the interstate, I turn onto the open road, bearing north towards the Crags.

EPILOGUE·

The journey back to Sydney was a quiet one, filled with reflections on the unexpected turns my life had taken.

Leaving Carmichael felt like closing a chapter, one that had taught me more about resilience and hope than I could have imagined. As the familiar skyline of Sydney came into view, I felt a sense of coming home, not just to a place, but to a new version of myself. My brief stay with Charlie gave me time and distance to think about time in Carmichael and being with Drew, his friends, and Lara. I am embarrassed to admit I hadn't wanted to help them, hadn't even wanted them there. But looking back, I wouldn't have changed a thing. The time with them has meant so much and has brought me out of my head so that now, coming home this time, I feel a thousand times lighter than when I had left.

And I thought about Lara. A lot. I understood her reasons for not wanting more than a friendship, and I would never press her to accept more, but there was a definite chemistry between us that assured me that not now didn't mean never. Who knew what could be in store for us?

Although the trip stretched out much longer than I'd planned, every extra day made me feel more optimistic about my future. Josh had a plan for a new business, and I was excited to hear more about it. He'd called earlier, and I told him I was at Lizzie's, and he said he'd be right over. I was in my sister's backyard, playing with George, when I heard the gate click and swing open. I looked up to see Josh entering the yard, and I waved him over. He took a seat on the top step behind me and a little to my left so as to dodge the playful onslaught of foam darts from George's toy gun.

There was little chance of any dart finding its way to us, as I had George pinned behind a tree. I was keeping him there with a barrage of foam missiles from my rocket launcher, and I had enough to keep him there for a long time.

"I don't think you're being fair to the nephew, Bro," Josh hit me on the arm lightly and chuckled.

"Fair? This is war. He doesn't get fair," I said, and I sent more rapid fire at the tree, the foam darts bouncing off the bark and covering the grass. George giggled from his position behind the giant, ancient oak tree, and I pulled the priming slide back on my blaster to load more foam darts. I had an endless supply.

Josh picked up a larger blaster, one that seemed to use bigger, fatter foam missiles, and aimed it at me, hitting me in the neck and back. I jumped off the steps and ran into the middle of the yard as Josh continued pulling the trigger, the missiles bouncing off me, giving George a chance to run.

"You're dead, Uncle Sean. Uncle Josh got you." George squealed, running over to hide behind Josh.

"Alright, buddy, he got me. But I'm badly wounded, but I'm not dead yet," I yelled, bringing up my blaster and sending darts at both George and Josh. Josh returned fire, hitting me every time while George tried to load his blaster. He was laughing hysterically and couldn't hold on to his darts.

"Dude, you're dead now," Josh yelled, shielding George. "You've gotta give up,"

"You got him, Uncle Josh. I ran out of ammunition, but you got him." Red in the face, hot and sweaty, George plopped down on the back stairs between Josh's feet, huffing and puffing. I walked over to join them, grabbed three bottles of water out of the cooler, and I also sat on the steps. After passing them a bottle of water and opening mine, I gave my friend a pointed look.

"I was winning until you came," I said reprovingly.

"You were taking advantage of the nephew," Josh said, slinging an arm around the sweaty boy and giving him a manly, one-armed hug. George grinned. He was happy to be hanging out with his two favorite people. Then I heard Lizzie calling George from inside the house.

"Dude, go eat lunch. We'll be right here," I tapped George on the shoulder, and he went inside, leaving me and Josh to talk. "Since we'll be saving the world, I presume you've brought over my cape and tights, yeah?" I asked, turning to Josh with a chuckle.

"Nah, but we will need a few new business suits. They might be a little more effective in the boardroom, at least in the begin-ning. Later, once we're up and running, we'll mostly be onsite, surveying old mines and quarries," Josh replied, handing me a thick sheaf of papers. I'd read everything he'd sent me on the industry, but scanning the stack of papers, this was all of the financials for our business venture. I liked those figures.

"So, you say we'll be in the business of turning old coal and mineral mines, diamond mines, and quarries into useful land for farming and development?"

"Exactly, it's called environmental remediation," Josh said.

"We can make this kind of money doing it?" I asked, fanning the edge of the papers with my thumb.

"Lots. And that's just in Brenner Industrials' backyard. Some governments and organizations are clamoring for this technology. They need more land and more housing developments for their people. But first, we need a lot of seed money to get started. It's for the technology and expertise. We'll have recouped it inside a year."

"And you've got the funds?"

"Kinda. We're going to get it from Brenner Industrials."

"You're going to ask your Dad?"

"No. We're going to present our business proposition to him and the board. One he won't refuse."

"Why not?"

"It would look bad in the press. Besides, Ian's helping me with the details. You and I are meeting him tomorrow."

"Okay. Count me in."

I laughed, shoving Josh playfully, and he pushed me back, practically sending me off the steps. I turned and blasted Josh in the chest with several foam darts, and he retaliated with his foam rocket blaster, sending fat foam missiles at me as I sprinted down the steps and out into the yard. We were both laughing so hard that it startled George, who peeked out the back door.

"Are you okay, Uncle Sean?" George called out.

"Yeah, Buddy, I'm fine," I gasped, lying out in the grass in the center of the yard.

"You're a lunatic," Josh declared.

"You are a genius. Walk me through everything again. I want to hear every single detail again," I said, catching my breath.

"Now?" Josh asked.

"Right now," I replied with enthusiasm.

Josh grinned. He knew I would find this business idea intriguing. Like him, I needed something that I could sink my teeth into. We continued to sit on the back steps of Lizzie's house until the sun began to set, outlining our strategies. At that moment, I realized that our bond, forged when we were ten years old, the moment we became best friends, had been strengthened by the challenges of adulthood and was unbreakable.

Leaving the surf circuits wasn't the end of everything but rather the beginning of something new.

Acknowledgments

Thank you for delving into the pages of *Wild Tides*, the second installment of the *Summer Adrift* series. I trust you found Sean's perspective an engaging addition to the narrative. This series has been a labor of love, and its realization owes gratitude to the unwavering support and assistance of numerous individuals who have accompanied me on this journey. To them, I extend my sincerest appreciation for their faith in both me and the book.

To you, the reader, I extend my heartfelt gratitude for your interest in and connection with the tales spun within these pages. My family deserves special recognition for their patience and understanding during the long hours and late nights devoted to bringing these stories to life. In particular, I am profoundly grateful to my daughter, Erika—my foremost advocate and confidante, who has served as reader, editor, champion, and a constant source of encouragement through every stage of this endeavor. Without her unwavering support, this book might still be confined to the depths of my computer's files.

Furthermore, I express my profound appreciation to my beta readers, whose invaluable feedback helped shape this story into its best form. Your insights and critiques have been instrumental in refining this narrative. My gratitude knows no bounds, and I am deeply indebted to every one of you.

You can continue reading to catch a sneak peek into the third installment of the *Summer Adrift* series, *Inherit The Tides*.

E V McMillan.

Inherit The Tides
Summer Adrift

E V McMillan

Color Your World Press, 2024

Storytelling is not what I do for a living—it is how I do all that I do while I am living
~Donald Davis

To my family and friends, whose strength and spirit mirror the resilience of the waves—ever inspiring and endlessly renewing.

CHAPTER ONE·

Biarritz, France,
Four months earlier

It was already promising to be another unseasonably hot day.

The sky was striated with color, the rising sun having clawed away much of the purple darkness of the night, leaving streaks of blue, pink and gold. However, it was having less success vanishing the oppressive humidity and thick, dark-gray marine layer that threatened a deluge of rain. It was only the end of May when temps should have been much more moderate, but global warming had settled over this idyllic seaside resort. An unprecedented number of tourists, surfers, and fans had converged on the town just as temps skyrocketed far beyond the highest numbers ever recorded, yet this morning, it was perfect for getting out and stretching my legs.

I left the sandy beach and walked along the main promenade fronted with quaint shops and cafes and followed the cliffside road up toward the residential heart of the town. The sound of the ocean, a constant, soothing rumble in the background, gradually faded, and the salt air mingled with the intoxicating perfume of flowers in full bloom. Vibrant bougainvillea, jasmine, lavender, hydrangeas, and wild roses lined the pathways and adorned the quaint balconies of the residences I passed. The morning slowly came alive with the symphony of everyday life: the soft chatter of early risers exchanging greetings, the clinking of dishes and the soft bark of orders from behind the half-open kitchen doors of a nearby café, and the distant bark of a dog. All were set against the quiet hum of a town waking up.

I stopped at the top of the slope, where the quiet road ended, intersecting with a much busier road, heavy traffic flowing to and from the heart of the town. I turned to look back towards the ocean, gaining a bird's eye view of the coast. The sight was a feast for the eyes. Charming Basque houses with their traditional red and white facades stood proudly amidst modern villas boasting sleek lines and expansive glass windows, a blend of the old and the new, much like the city of Biarritz itself. In a few hours, the serene tranquility of early morning will transform into a pulsating hive of activity. The narrow, twisty streets offering a peaceful stroll will thrum with an energy so tangible it will feel like an electric current in the air. And these calm pathways will converge into a raging river of humanity as surfers, fans, tourists, and residents stream toward the water in a colorful, chaotic dance. Gone will be the gentle symphony of morning routines, replaced by the excited chatter of crowds and the shouts of vendors selling surf gear and local delicacies. Gone will be the constant, rhythmic thumping of music from beachside bars and cafes, and the air, now filled with the soft scent of flowers and sea salt, will carry a mix of sunscreen, street food, and the adrenaline of anticipation.

For three days, competitors and spectators have gathered on the pristine white sand of this exotic French enclave. The ocean, a canvas of the deepest blues and greens, has offered up waves that surfers dream of—a flawless combination of power, height, and rhythm as if Neptune himself had ordained this place to be the arena for such a prestigious competition. Three days in which athletes commanded the waves with grace and power, dancing atop the crests with the very essence of the sea, each turn and aerial a tribute to the beauty and power of this untamed force of nature. And every rider had been rewarded with applause and shouts, the collective breath of spectators held and released with every successful maneuver and every heartbreaking wipeout.

This was my third time in Biarritz but my second time competing in the International Tourney. Colin, our coach and mentor, had prepared the five of us, the guppies on the team, that we would unlikely walk away with any honors in our division, but it was one of the best training grounds for us to hone our skills. None of us had advanced beyond the second-level elimination heats, but we celebrated nonetheless and with great enthusiasm. Today was the last day. We would watch from the sidelines as Josh, our team captain, prevailed.

All afternoon yesterday, Josh had battled against waves that seemed to encapsulate the spirit of the Tourney. Raging waves seemed to recognize the importance of the occasion, pushing the ten competitors to the limits of their abilities. The heats had ended with Josh a fraction of a point behind the reigning, three-time champion Piper Lewis. Each advance had been hard won, each ride breath-taking. If he continued the day as he ended yesterday, he could dethrone Lewis, taking the title of *Ultimate Surfer.*

Taking a deep breath and feeling a smile tug across my face, I started back down the road, back toward the beach and the hotel, where my teammates—my family—were likely waking up and getting ready for the day. While most of the team would be packing up and scattering to points unknown, my mates and I would only have to move less than a half kilometer away to a small-ish Villa we'd planned to rent for a month. *Villa Coeur de la Mer*, which translates to *Heart of the Sea Villa*, sat on the edge of the ocean. The property was so completely self-sufficient and encompassing that we wouldn't have to go outside the grounds for food or recreation, no matter how long we stayed. We were excitedly looking forward to spending the next few weeks enjoying everything it had to offer.

~

We'd only been on vacation for two nearly weeks and already we'd burned through every activity on our month-long bucket list. The five of us, Jordan Smith, Grayson Pierce, Joey Maldonado, Lloyd Carter, and myself, made the most of every day and every night. We'd gone surfing and paragliding, hiking, and mountain biking, taken in a couple of rugby matches, done a little golfing—though not very well, and taken a day trip to the historic city of Bayonne. Every evening, we'd return to the Villa, shower, change and head back out to immerse ourselves in the nightlife scene, where we met beautiful local women as well as tourists on holiday. I doubt I've ever felt so carefree and enjoyed myself so much.

After more than a week of non-stop activity, it didn't take much to convince us to spend one evening at the Villa, chopping it up around the huge stone fireplace, a snapping and crackling fire burning inside. Warmth wrapped the large common room in a comforting embrace, keeping out the unseasonable chill of the light, drizzly rain that had descended on the town. And though we still had another two weeks left, we were already starting to look forward to getting back on the water and reuniting with the rest of the team. We were expected to meet up with everyone in Peniche, Portugal. Josh, Sean and Colin would have cut their vacation short so that Josh could fly out to Jo'berg to deal with sponsors, and Colin could spend some time in New South Wales, Australia with his family. Sean and Jeff would no doubt make a detour to conquer the Banzai Pipeline in Oahu—again, before meeting us in Peniche. Marc and Vince were on the East Coast, in North Carolina and Florida, respectively, spending time with family. Strangely enough, I missed them all. A month was the longest we'd all been apart in the three years I'd been with the team, the first real vacation any of us had in all that time, but I, for one, was looking forward to all of us getting back together.

Sated from a heavy dinner of meat and pasta with a thick cheese sauce that was now my new favorite, fresh-baked bread and drinks, we'd kicked back in companionable silence. Some-one was streaming American pop music on their phone when, suddenly, our phones began pinging. While it normally wasn't cause for alarm since most of us had an alert or two set to notify us whenever anything about our team or team members was mentioned on social media, it was unusual that so many alerts were going off at the same time. Lloyd was the first to open his news feed to breaking news. He drew a horrified breath and showed us several grainy photos of a surfer lying in the sand, a tourniquet wrapped around his leg splashed up the news app. He eerily looked like Josh. The caption read; *Joshua Alan Brenner, elite surfer and son of Australian billionaire James Brenner, titan and CEO of Brenner Industrials, attacked in a freak shark attack off the coast of San Diego.*

We quickly opened our own phones and skimmed the plethora of articles, though most had scant details of the attack and his condition. We also started calling and texting Josh, Colin, Sean—anyone and everyone we could think of, though our messages went directly to voice mail. We sat together for hours, reading every bit of news on the internet that we could find.

The next morning, as we decided to pack up and find flights out to California, we received instructions from Jeff and Vince. Jeff assured us that the accident was, in fact, every bit as bad as had been reported and that there was nothing we could do in San Diego. He also let us know that while in critical condition, the doctors were confident Josh would pull through. He also let us know Sean was fine but had no news on Colin. Vince called immediately afterward, telling us to sit tight and that he and Marc were catching a flight out to us. We had no idea why they wanted us to remain halfway around the globe when we wanted to be in the States, but we did as they asked, hanging together in the

Villa, worrying, and waiting. We figured it would take them at least 15 hours to fly into Paris and then on to Biarritz.

The next evening, more than seventy-two hours after receiving the first report of the accident, the heavy, sonorous sound of the doorbell echoing throughout the Villa brought us all rushing down to the common room. Malcolm, the household manager, who acted as the steward, butler, valet, and housekeeper, was already greeting Vince and Marc by the time I made it down from my room. They had all of their gear in tow and looked like they'd aged at least a decade. Their usual stoke dialed down to zero; their whole vibe was so far off the charts that I knew things had to be even worse than we'd imagined.

We pulled them into the common room while Malcolm handled their gear. There was more than enough room in the Villa for them to stay, and we were happy enough to have them there and in charge. We dropped like stones onto the sofas and chairs, practically holding our breath. Silence filled the room like a heavy fog as we stared at them, hoping the news wasn't as bad as what we'd conjured up in our imagination. Vince, the elder guru of our crew—not just in years but in pure wisdom and surf soul, attempted to clear his voice several times. It was clear that he was having difficulty dropping the bomb on us.

"Guys, I'm sorry to have to have to bring this to you, but I need everyone to listen," he started, his usual chill replaced by this gnarly hesitation that wasn't his style, and his words were heavy, like a big wave set on the horizon. My heart sank, catching this wave of dread.

"You know about the accident. Josh and Colin…," he barely got out, voice low, and the room felt like it shrunk, the air thinning out. "Josh is in the hospital, hanging on but critical. The doctors expect him to pull through, but Colin…" Vince's voice broke, showing cracks we never saw. "Colin didn't make it."

Didn't make it? Those words were like a wipeout, each one a hit that knocked the wind out of me. Josh, our star, battling for his life? And Colin, the rock of our team, the dude who saw the spark in all of us, who pulled me into this world when I was just a grom fleeing from dark clouds? *He didn't make it?* That was unreal. Crazy. It couldn't be true.

"Tell us what happened?" Lloyd demanded, while Joey asked, "How could that happen?"

The questions that had filled our heads as we tried to make sense of the past seventy-two hours bombarded Vince, spilling fast and furiously until Marc held up a hand.

"They were in SoCal, and a freak shark attack went down. Josh suffered serious bites to his leg and thigh, and they think Colin…he never made it back to shore. They have no idea what happened to him. The authorities presume he drowned. His body hasn't been recovered."

"From who? Who did you hear this from?" My bro, Jordan, piped up.

"Sean. He was there. The three of them were together."

My sight blurred, tears breaking free and streaming down my face. My crew, we all felt it—shock, sorrow, huddling together for the dude who was our north star and for Josh, whose light was flickering.

"How does something like this even happen? How does Colin just...drown?" That was me, though I hardly recognized my own voice, trying to paddle through the fog, looking for some mistake in this tale. Vince just shook his head.

"Details are sketchy, but Sean caught enough of it to lay it out for us."

"And Sean? He made it?"

"Yeah. He made it."

"So, what's our next move?" I asked. "We going to Cali?"

"No. We're going to hang tight. Marc and I came here to fill you in, and we're all gonna camp here till we get the full picture from Sean or Jeff. Sean's with Josh. Josh's family is flying in, and Jeff's taking point on the search and handling Colin's scene."

I nodded, tears falling into my lap. I don't know how long I sat there, lost in my thoughts, staring at the empty space beside me where Colin would have sat, his laughter booming like rolling thunder, mercilessly teasing anyone and everyone. He had been more than a mentor to me; a father figure I had craved, the guiding hand that had steered me away from the path of resentment and anger that had been laid out by my own father and brother, a supportive brother and friend. His belief in me was a stark contrast to the physical and mental abuse I'd escaped when I'd run away from home all those years ago. Losing him felt like being adrift at sea without a compass. The grief that filled the room was a palpable force. Dark waters threatened to pull me under. The Villa, once a slice of paradise, now felt suffocating, as if the walls were closing in. I stood up and walked away, though it was an unconscious act. Vince's hand found my shoulder, a grounding force in the tumult of emotions, and I stopped and looked up.

"We're going to get through this, Quinn," he said, his voice firm despite the tremor of emotion. "Together. It's what Colin would have wanted and what Sean and Josh expect. We're a team, in and out of the water."

I think I nodded, and he turned back to continue addressing questions from the group. I needed space to think, to be alone, and headed for the hall and the stairs to my room on the second floor. The pain I felt from Colin's loss was excruciating, made even more so because of how much I looked up to him, and I didn't hear Jordan, my closest friend, catch up with me at the foot of the stairs.

"You okay, Quinn?" he asked, putting his hand on my arm.

"I dunno. I can't believe it."

"I know. I can't either. Colin was an excellent swimmer. How could he just drown?"

I could hear the pain in his voice, and I turned to clasp his shoulder, giving it a firm squeeze. He and I were kindred spirits, though to look at us, we were like night and day. He was brown-skinned with sharp features and of Afro-Caribbean descent though he never claimed any island country as home. He had this whole laid-back, island-style going on with a discernible musical lilt to his speech, thick dreadlocks that he wore either tied back in a bunch or wrapped up on top of his head, an infectious smile that could light up a room.

In contrast, I was white, born and raised in Northern California, amongst endless sunshine, golden beaches, and the whole West Coast vibe. You could have been fooled into thinking I'd always been a laid-back, golden boy, but my reality was far from that postcard image. We had similar hard-knock backgrounds. Growing up, my family had scraped by day to day. My father, a devout and hard-working man, was also stern, closed-minded, and set in his thinking. He felt it was his duty to shake my head out of the clouds and see my shortcomings, and if hard work, severe scoldings or verbal reprimands wouldn't work, then he was confident his belt would. Maybe he was right; considering how hard it was to make ends meet, we could little afford daydreams.

Danny, my older brother, had enlisted in the Marines right after high school but was kicked out within a month of completing boot camp. He'd said it was because of a misunderstanding, but one severe enough to get him a dishonorable discharge. With nowhere else to go, he returned home and took out his frustrations in ways that left me more familiar with his meaty fists and the ground than I cared to admit.

My mother, *Bless her*, had tried to shield me from the beatings as best she could, but there was only so much she could do. My breaking point came just a few days shy of my high school graduation. I'd gone surfing with my friends, spending most of the day with them, and we'd stayed well into the evening, enjoying the crowd of kids drawn by the loud music and a huge bonfire. When I got home, my father was waiting for me, furious that I'd been gone all day instead of helping him and doing an honest day's work. My brother had taken advantage of my father's anger to punch me around again for some slight I'd unknowingly committed. Between the two, I could hardly stand on my own, much less walk, but I packed my few things in my backpack, grabbed my board, and left.

Homelessness was a brutal education in adaptation and survival. If I were to survive on my own, I could not allow myself to be taken advantage of. I had to make my own way. That's when surfing became less of a hobby and an escape from everyday life and my lifeline. I was good, and I loved surfing. It was the only skill I had, and I hung around, challenging anyone to surfing contests so that I'd have money to feed myself and buy the things I needed.

I met Colin while hustling surfing matches on the beach. I challenged him to a contest, and he bet me a hundred dollars that I couldn't beat him. He won the bet; he was so far out of my league, but I also won. He'd seen spirit, determination and potential in a kid with nothing but a beat-up surfboard and a heart full of ambition. And he didn't just pick me up and teach me how to refine my surfing technique; he showed me how to channel my dreams into something tangible, something real. Under his guidance and the competitiveness and friendship of Jordan and Gray, surfing became my passion and my path.

Our backgrounds, Jordan's and mine were marked by hardship and abuse, and it became the backbone of our resilience and determination. I learned that being a dreamer wasn't a flaw but the very thing that could save you. And that family isn't always the one you're born into but one you choose from the people who care about you and accept you.

I don't know if I slept once I lay across my bed, but as the rain ended and dawn approached, the reality of our loss and the battle ahead had settled heavily upon me. I knew the path forward would be unclear, fraught with the pain of Colin's absence and the uncertainty of Josh's fate. I didn't know if we would still be a team or what our next steps were going to be, but I was ready to do whatever the team needed us to do.

The days blurred together, one indistinguishable from the next. We rarely left the Villa, spending our days in the common room, the epicenter of our vigil. The television, the sound muted, was constantly tuned to the news channels. We consumed every scrap of information about Josh or Colin like starving men, yet with each passing day, the silence from the other side of the globe grew louder, a gaping void filled with our worst fears.

Only a few weeks ago, the Villa, with its sprawling rooms and sunlit spaces, had been an idyllic retreat. The future had seemed as bright and limitless as the azure blue skies and turquoise ocean, and laughter had been our constant companion. Now, it felt as though the walls themselves mourned. The light was too harsh, the shadows were too deep, and every sound was too loud. We moved through the rooms like ghosts, our conversations a series of whispers and heavy silences. But no one spoke of leaving, not even for food. The thought of missing a call or an update on Josh's condition or Colin's situation anchored us to the Villa with a weight heavier than grief. The outside world, with its relentless march forward, seemed a distant reality we were all too willing to ignore. Our focus became singular—any news of Colin and any word on Josh's fight for life.

The blue gleaming pool went untouched, its sparkling waters a stark reminder of a joy we could no longer grasp. The tennis and pickleball courts and our surfboards were ignored; the thought of having fun, of hitting the waves without Colin's laughter ringing in our ears, or the anticipation of Josh's triumphant return felt like a betrayal.

I wandered to the balcony in the early hours before dawn. Below, the ocean whispered promises of continuity, of waves that would keep coming long after we were gone. It was a comfort and a curse, a reminder of the impermanence of our troubles but also of the deep loss we had suffered.

Then, after more than a month of uncertainty and grief, Vince called us into a huddle. His voice, though heavy with the weight we all felt, was firm and decisive. "Time to get our heads back in the game," he said, locking eyes with each of us. "We've got waves to catch, for Josh, for Colin. They wouldn't want us bailing now. We need to honor them the best way we know how. Pack it up. We have a flight to catch."

His words were a beacon, cutting through the fog. We're surfers, heart and soul, with a lineup calling our names. The Villa, our refuge, had become a prison of our own making, a place where time stood still and grief was our only companion.

That night, we began to gather up all of our belongings, and the next day, we were rolling out. Taghazout, Morocco, was our next stop on the league's itinerary, and we all felt like we were leaving a piece of us behind. However, the stoke slowly returned, mixed with grit, gratitude, and the drive to keep our legacy alive. Our job was far from over. Grief would accompany us, a noiseless, hovering specter that may never fully recede, but so too would the courage Colin had cultivated in us, the determination that Josh exemplified in every competition, and the resilience we'd share with one another in the coming days, weeks, and months. As a team, we've always had a bond, but now it was solid, forged in the hottest fires of loss and grief and tempered in the deepest waters of brotherhood and commitment. We were ready, one and all, to do what we did best.

CHAPTER TWO

Southern California, USA
September

We arrived at LAX in the early afternoon, and after navigating customs and baggage claim procedures, I followed my mates outside to the coach bus boarding area.

The heat and humidity immediately enveloped us like a sauna. The sky was still overcast from the rain that had drenched the city earlier. I slung my duffel over my shoulder, and trying to dodge the deepest of puddles, I headed to where our coach bus was waiting. I plopped down near the back of the bus, though there was plenty of room for the eight of us occupying it. Vince, Jeff, and Marc were in hushed conversation up front, near the driver. Jordan, Joey, and Lloyd, in full chat mode, making terrible jokes and teasing one another, took seats in the middle of the bus. Gray stretched out over two seats across from me, pulling his baseball cap down over his eyes. I decided to emulate him and catch a few Zs as well. The bus lurched into motion, tossing us around violently enough to rattle our teeth before smoothing out on the tarmac road.

I was glad to be back in the States and in Huntington Beach. We usually get to Southern California once a year, and this time we were hoping to meet up with Sean and Josh for the first time since the accident four months ago. It would be good to see them again. Josh had had a helluva close call and was lucky to get away with his life. That shark was on him like he was some kind of tasty treat, and he was in a bad way when Sean got him out of the water. Sean, along with Josh's family, had been able to come and go at the hospital, and he had been righteous about keeping us in the loop on Josh's recovery and rehab. He was also solid at clarifying the truth buried in the media's crazy stories. For weeks, the internet had blown up with all the drone and cellphone footage, and the media circus that followed kept the story alive.

It still gutted me that Colin had never been found, but I was grateful that Sean had shared Colin's gear with us. Some of the guys used the things they received, hoping it would be good Karma when they competed, but I felt it was good Karma just having some of it. Most of what I'd received was stored in a locker in Vista Valley, a town about ten miles from where my parents lived.

Despite, or maybe because of the gravity of the situation, none of us bailed on the competitions. We'd pushed through the rest of the tour, competing in our scheduled events, winning and losing as a squad. We'd just finished up a rough two-week run. Ten days ago, we were shredding it up in Banyu Wangi, Indonesia, where we'd lost our shirts and our dignity. From there, we went directly to Playa Ricon in the Dominican Republic, and yesterday, we'd finished a four-day meet in Teahupo'o Tahiti. Last night, we drove a couple of hours to Papeete, Tahiti's capital city, to catch our midnight flight.

The rhythm of the bus on the highway was a lullaby. I didn't even realize I'd drifted off until Gray roughly nudged me awake. We'd rolled up to our crash pad, the Cielo De Mar Hotel. It was fancy, as always. We were five-star everywhere we went. I shouldered my duffel and my gear, followed everyone off the bus, and headed straight for the hotel lobby. Snagging my room key, I heard s few of the others buzzing about food and a night out. When they asked me to join them, I took a pass. The plan for me was simple—a hot shower and a soft bed. I was ready to crash.

The next morning, feeling way more human, I walked into a lobby swarming with the who's who of the surf world—riders, reps, reporters. It was like stepping into a beehive of cameras and chitchat, but I saw the guys sitting in a restaurant on the lanai and joined them. I pulled up a chair and scooched in between Joey and Gray.

"Did you get enough rest, Sleeping Beauty?" Gray teased me.

"Of course. You know I need my beauty rest." I shot back.

"Well, maybe you need a few more hours," Joey said with a smirk.

"Dude, no matter how much sleep you get, it doesn't seem to make a difference." I retorted.

"That's because I can get no prettier!"

We all laughed. Joey is an arrogant ass but he's *our* arrogant ass. I flagged the server down and placed my order for a huge breakfast. It felt like my stomach was so empty my belly button was sticking to my spine.

"I got a text from Sean that he and Josh should be here around noon. They're driving up from San Diego." Jeff volunteered.

"Do you think Sean's going to participate in the meet?" I asked.

"Haven't heard differently."

I nodded. Sean would bring in some needed cash. No one would beat him now that Josh was out, and one check from him would likely beat all the money the rest of us would earn. Besides, it was always exciting watching him take on the waves. We chatted about random things until three servers came out carrying our food. I started on the pancakes, drowning them in strawberry syrup as soon as they were set down in front of me.

Having moved from the restaurant to the seating area on the other side of the lanai, we'd sat around chilling until we saw Sean pull up in a convertible, with Josh grinning from the passenger seat. Hotel staff swooped in to grab their gear and park the car. We all got up to greet them as they made their way to the lobby. I locked on Josh, trying to get a read on him, checking him to see if anything was different. He was moving a bit gingerly on his left side, but, man, he looked good—tanned and way stronger than I'd been braced for. Seeing him like that, standing tall and unbroken, greeting us with a touch and a handshake, was like the biggest weight taken off my shoulders. He looked solid, and I was relieved to see him like that.

I followed them inside, feeling the stoke coming off everyone as people suddenly recognized them. The energy in the room spiked off the chart as people crowded around them, dozens of voices becoming an excited roar. It was crazy. Josh was like the main attraction, Sean moving aside so the team and everyone else could get his attention. He was all smiles, high-fives, and bro-hugs, even though you could tell he'd probably kill for a chance to give his leg a rest. I gave a mental nod to his cool handling of the mob. He was a natural with people, outgoing and charismatic, never ignoring or turning anyone away. I saw Sean move out of the limelight, noting how chill he was compared to Josh, like brothers, but like night and day. Sean was always in the background, running things, keeping things moving like a well-oiled machine. He seldom mugged for the shutter-hounds, though they probably followed him as much as they followed Josh. I think our brand was as tight as a bank vault because of the way Sean handled things. He wasn't the kind of person to make decisions rashly.

Vince, Marc and Jeff joined Sean on the sidelines, where they could keep one eye on Josh. I guess the three of them were Josh's de facto bodyguards, as they were always in place to push back the crowds that usually tried to form too tightly around him. Though they were alert, they seemed content enough to chop it up on the sidelines. I cut through the crowd and went to stand beside Sean, who flipped around, all smiles, and hit me with a firm clasp on the shoulder.

"How's it going, Quinn?"

"Keeping it together, Sean. How about you?"

"Good, good. You alright?" asking after my well-being that went beyond the moment. I nodded.

"Yeah, I'm okay. Thanks for sending me Colin's gear. I don't know how to tell you how much that meant to me."

"I already know, Quinn. You guys were like little brothers to him. You were as important to him as he was to you."

"Still, I just appreciate you for looking out."

"Of course, man. You all checked in?" Again, I nodded, and he gave my shoulder a squeeze. Turning back to Jeff and Vince, he said, "I'm ready to get some grub. How about we meet in twenty?"

"Yeah, sounds good. The Dolphin Room?" Vince asked. They'd apparently been making plans before I showed up. Sean nodded and glanced over at Josh. The dude looked pretty wiped despite the big grin on his face, and Marc broke off from us to disperse the crowd.

"Heads up, everyone," Jeff shouted, his voice carrying across the lobby. "We're rallying in the Dolphin Room in twenty for some grub and a huddle, yeah? Josh and Sean need to shoot up to their rooms before they meet us there. Any questions, see Vince."

Sean clapped me on the back again and moved away, heading towards the bank of elevators. Vince and I watched Marc break up the crowd around Josh so he could disentangle himself from the well-wishers and head for the elevators. With a big grin on his face, Vince grabbed me in a one-armed headlock, squeezing me against his side and laughing raucously. Jeff, seeing me helpless, came back over and jabbed me twice, one to the bicep, following up with one in the side, while Vince kept me locked in his armpit. I apparently was to be their punching bag for the afternoon.

"I was keen on just sipping my lunch, but I guess I could munch on a little something too," Jeff said, finally stepping back, though he gave me another jab to the ribs. Vince just shot a look from him to me and shrugged. Without a word, he released me and bailed, likely heading to the Dolphin Room, leaving me disheveled and none too steady. Jeff followed him, flexing his biceps and laughing loudly.

~

The Dolphin Room was a small private dining and conference room with large windows facing a long stretch of ocean and sandy beach. The heavy black-out drapes were pulled aside, letting in bright afternoon sunlight. Lunch was an assortment of sandwiches and cold salads, which we scarfed down quickly. We listened avidly as Josh and Sean shared everything they'd been through over the last few months. We even had an opportunity to tease Josh for falling in love with the doctor who had saved him. Though we teased him, we were massively happy for him.

When the food was cleared away, Jordan picked up his glass and tapped it to get everyone's attention. We turned to him, giving him our undivided attention, even though I knew what was coming next. Anxiety began to bubble up in my stomach.

"So, check this," he said, his dark brown eyes flashing, his voice rich and smooth. "Quinn and I have been thinking… what if we hit the waves for a paddle-out tonight?" It was more of a statement than a question. "We know Colin's folks had a private service for him back in Australia, but most of us missed out. Doing it together would be solid—for the team."

Silence fell over the table as everyone weighed the idea. I caught a glimpse of Josh's face tense up, then smooth over just as quick.

"Can we get enough flower leis in such a short time?" Sean asked, sounding like he might be in.

"We can probably get enough for us, but we'll see how many extra we can get."

"Tonight's the only shot we got, what with tomorrow being go-time, from sunup to sundown, there won't be another chance." Jordan was quick to add. "It won't matter if it's just us. He was our Bro, our rock."

"And what's the play? Keep it just us, or are we opening this up to whoever's down for it?" Marc asked.

I smiled. I could feel my anxiety fading. "Anyone…everyone is welcome. I'm sure a few people will want to come and honor him."

"The more, the merrier," Jordan added. Everyone started nodding, and we got the nod from Sean to make it happen. Just like that, it was on. Sunset paddle-out tonight, open invite.

By evening, what started as a ten-man send-off had blown up. Maybe a hundred or more people showed up, and Jordan and I passed out the extra leis we'd purchased to the drop-ins who hadn't thought to bring one. We paddled out on our boards, leis clenched in our teeth, making our way to a spot where Jordan waited. We sat cross-legged on our boards and joined hands to form a massive circle. In circular formation, we placed the flowers on the water inside the circle formed by the noses of our boards, chanted, splashed, and churned the water. We stuck candles on the nose of our boards and lit them just as the sun descended and twilight gathered and spoke a few words in honor of Colin. Prayers were offered, and blessings implored, and in less than an hour, it was over. It had been a moving ceremony, and as darkness fell upon us, we turned around and headed back to shore, many of us feeling closure for the first time.

Feeling surprisingly good afterward, and on my way back to my room, I picked up a couple different magazines strategically spread around the lobby. They were even stacked up at each end of the reception and concierge desks for guests to pick up. I recognized our P.R. firm's fingerprints all over the ploy since Josh's picture was on the front of most of them–either bold, front and center or small and placed along the side. I took a couple of them with me, and once inside my room, I plopped down in the deep, comfortable chair in front of the windows, cracked a bottle of water from the small in-room fridge, and began perusing the articles.

A full portrait of Josh graced the cover of the June issue of *Surf Rider*, weeks after Josh won the *Ultimate Surfer* title in Biarritz back in May. The content of the article was familiar. All the journalists wrote the same thing, but I checked out the pictures included. There were at least a dozen high-def photos of all of us mugging for the camera. Me and Jordan and Colin, look-ing totally extreme–Colin with his bright ginger locks catching fire in the sun, me with my dark, almost black hair pulled into a wolf's tail, and Jordan's locs in shades from bright gold to dark mahogany pulled up in a bunch looking very Bob Marley-like. The only thing we had in common were our huge smiles, all teeth and gums because we were cheesing so hard.

There was an action shot of Sean running out of the ocean, surfboard in hand, after his heats, his long black hair catching the breeze, whipping and snapping behind him, and another of Col-in jumping around on the sand, obviously excited about whatev-er had just taken place. Colin was short compared to Sean and built like a wrestler, while Sean was tall and slim, graceful and supremely agile. Colin had been a gentle bear. Not a Teddy bear, but more like Father Bear.

At the end of the article, there was a shot that zoomed in on Sean, Colin and Josh talking in a huddle and another of the entire team, all of us seated in the sand, in front of our boards, which were standing upright in the sand. They were probably some of the last shots taken of Colin and certainly the last of all of us together. We'd been super stoked after those big wins in the Ultimate Surfer event in Biarritz. Immediately after, Josh, Sean, and Colin took off for their long-awaited vacation and the horror that awaited them.

The next couple of sports magazines carried the story of the shark attack. I flipped through those pictures, not wanting to fo-cus much on the grizzly pictures. I'd been traumatized enough watching the story in real time. The last magazine carried the story and a few pictures of Josh doing rehab, including a photo of a cute woman doctor in scrubs and a lab coat, standing by his side. She supposedly was the one to have saved his life. Dr. Mia Thomas, the caption stated. It was a nice, proof of life picture of him, as he tried to walk holding on to parallel bars. She was beaming like he'd stolen home base. I closed the magazine, tossing it along with the rest onto the desk. Housekeeping would collect them in the morning.

CHAPTER
THREE

Opening day was electric.

Sean was tipped to take it all in the Men's Masters Division, and just having him there with us had the whole team jacked up. We were all buzzing, especially the squads gunning for the big kahuna and the Champion's Cup. The lineup was stacked—forty-four crews deep. Some teams were rolling three deep, but our gang had a solid four: Sean was back on the roster, and Vince had stepped up to the number two spot, filling in Colin's slot. Then Marc, followed by Joey Maldonado. Joey had hustled hard to snag that last open slot, beating out me, Jordon, Grayson, and Lloyd. At nineteen, Joey was the youngest on the team, but he wasn't called Cowboy for nothing. He was a real hustler and a show-off and had the skill and talent to back up his bravado. While we all had talent and skill, Joey was fearless. Thrill rides were his bread and butter, and we needed a little of his thrill-seeking to wow the judges if we were going to take the division honors.

Like most big competitions, the days were a mix of hurry-up-and-wait. Team and individual events were full-throttle, heart-pounding action interspersed with lots of waiting. Fourteen divisions were competing in total, with two hundred or more athletes at the top of their game. There were two and four-person team events for the Junior Men and Women, the Intermediate

Men and Women, and the Advanced Men and Women on the first two days. Then, the Individual Men's and Women's events, at the same three levels, took place on the second and third day. On the last day and a half, the Championship Men's and Women's events took place. Many competitors participated in multiple events at varying levels.

I had competed in the two-person team and the men's individual intermediate event. I had survived the elimination heats and would be back on the waves that afternoon. But in the meantime, I was at the shoreline, hanging out in knee-deep froth, cheering on my crew that were still competing. When the spray settled, our boys had crushed it, carving their names into the next lineup.

Josh was there, too, but not to shred. He was working the charm offensive for the sponsors and building up the hype, doing his bit on the sidelines. I caught a glimpse of his mug grinning from the jumbotron, chilling with the commentary crew—Kevin Collier, Lonnie Davis, and George Durant—because the crowd was going nuts. They loved him and showed it, their cheers like a wave of sound crashing over us. Josh lapped it up, stood tall, and gave a double-armed salute.

"Peep Josh hogging the limelight." Jeff jabbed me, thumbing back at the big screen.

"Playing the hype man? Not my scene," I said with a shake of my head. I couldn't begin to imagine myself giving an impromptu interview to thousands of people live and on television.

Jeff just chuckled. "It ain't too shabby when you're tight

with those boys."

Collier, the dude who used to rule the waves before he traded his surfboard for a mic, was dissecting plays like the pro he once was. And Davis's career had been cut short a few years back by a wack wipeout. That had been messed up. I remember going head-to-head with his team more than a few times before they broke up. Then there was Durant. He'd never shredded a wave competitively, but he climbed the media ladder to become the face of his own sports show.

Josh was killing it with them, looked like he was made for the camera—no shocker— and he was still riding the high from snagging his eighth World Title in Biarritz just a few months back. He had plenty to talk about.

On day two, we were all up with the dawn and buzzing, even though most of us had barely clocked any shut-eye. There were sixty bright-eyed souls lined up to throw down for our solo showdown, and I was itching to claim that big five-figure purse in the Men's Individuals. As we gathered, everyone's eyes were on the skies, gray and moody, with thick thunderheads shrouding the sun. For a while, it seemed like the competition might be paused, but after a long deliberation among the officials, the competitors were given the all-clear. The waves were beasts determined not to be conquered by mere mortals. The crowd had more than doubled, spilling from the cliffs down to the crush at the surf line. Security was hustling, keeping the onlookers at bay. My number was thirty-eight, a long wait in the wings, so I snagged a front-row seat to watch them pull aerials and slice up the waves with slick moves. They were my competition.

My turn was coming up soon when I heard a commotion a little further up the beach. I could see Jeff in the thick of it, his blond mop sticking above the crowd. Some others of our crew darted over, ready to dive into the melee, but I stayed put. My eyes were on the prize, not about to get sidetracked over a scuffle, even if it was Jeff stirring it up—again.

Within minutes, it seemed to get bigger and more disorderly, and I was hard-pressed to remain at the shoreline and stay focused. Surf. Scuffle. Surf…then I heard my number called. That was my cue. I shoved the beach drama to the back of my mind because it was showtime. I snagged my board and hit the water, paddling out to the lineup. Three ahead, two bobbing behind, all of us champing at the bit for our shot. When it's my turn, I meet the wave head-on. It's a beast, but I'm ready. I hunker down, find my line, and drop in just as the wave curls over, tucking me into its barrel. I'm in the pocket, riding the surge, battling to keep my edge.

Busting out of the barrel to the sight of sunlight winking off the water, I knew I nailed it—a stunner right off the bat. The buzz from that ride was unreal. I made my way to the beach, planted my board in the sand, and the props started rolling in—high fives and hoots from all over. My team, though? MIA. It was weird, sure, but my head was all about the next wave.

Despite kicking off with a bang, the rest of my runs fizzled. By the end, I was out of the running, with no cash to show for it. So, I headed back, feeling the sting of defeat. Walking into the hotel lobby, Vince caught me straight away. "Dude, where've you been?"

"Been at the beach, bro. Where else? What's the deal here?"

"Chaos, man. Beach brawl. We got snagged by security."

"It was Jeff, wasn't it?" I snapped. "He and his trap can't ever just lay low."

"Surprisingly, nope. Some journo got in Josh's grill, things got nasty, and Jeff, well, he went full knockout on the guy and his camera buddy. Place turned into a free-for-all, and next thing, we were all stuck at the pavilion. The big wigs were this close to axing us from the comp."

"Seriously? How'd you wiggle out of that mess?"

"Josh, man, he's slick. Must've cut some kind of deal. We're still on. But Jeff's on lockdown, banned from the beach till the comp's done."

"That's nuts," I said, shocked and disgusted.

"Totally. You weren't there. I figured you'd dodged the bullet."

"Missed it by a hair. I was in the solo run when it kicked off. Caught a glimpse, then it was my turn to ride."

"Rough out there?"

"Didn't make the cut for the prize." I shrugged it off like it was nothing, but it still stung.

"Shame, man. Some of the guys are gonna cut loose tonight and shake off the drama. You in?"

"Pass. Gonna rinse off the day and chill. How about you?"

"Still tossing it up. Might hit the town, might not."

"I'm going to pass. Catch you later."

"Sure thing. Later."

Riding the elevator up, I couldn't shake the image of the beach turning into a throwdown ring. Josh and a reporter? That was the last scene I'd expect. Reporters usually ate up whatever Josh dished out—not just because he's a champ a bunch of times over, but the guy's also rolling in it, splashed across every glossy mag worth a glance, and bankrolled by the sort of sponsors that make other surfers go green. What could've lit that fuse?

I had to get the lowdown, and Jordan was my go-to for the scoop—he had an ear in every conversation and eyes on every move. Once I got cleaned up, I was going to try to get all my questions answered.

~

The four days of events had gone as smoothly as butter, and the divisions were over. The final day dawned gloriously sunny, bright, and warm, and we were gathered on the beach for the final competition for the Championship Cup. The initial forty-odd contenders had boiled down to ten, with Sean top-seeded. Josh was MIA, but the rest of us were there to cheer him on for the win.

That evening, the hotel ballroom had been decorated for a sumptuous dinner and dancing, with exotic perfumed flowers and fruit arrangements as centerpieces and decorations. Over a hundred and fifty round-top tables covered in snow-white linens, crystal, and gold-rimmed China were spread throughout the room, the walls of windows were open to the night, and a massive, open double-sided fireplace to one side of the room threw enough warmth to counterbalance the breeze off the ocean. All of the conference attendees had tickets to dinner, a way to greet old friends and make new ones.

I'd come down a little early to look around the hotel, maybe prowl the gift shops and see what else there was to offer, but I ran into Lloyd and Jordan talking to a group of girls. They flagged me over and introduced me to the ladies, who were members of the Women's Surf Division. We chitchat for a few minutes, standing in the middle of the breezeway and thinking it might be better if we moved out of the way of pedestrian traffic. I asked the ladies if they'd like to find a table for dinner. We all sat together near the open expanse overlooking the lanai and the ocean beyond. Somehow, I ended up between two young ladies who seemed to be good friends.

Sarena was Brazilian from Rio, and she had a thick accent that was a little difficult to decipher as she chattered excitedly. The other one was named Carey, and she was from South Africa near the Cape. Both were on the same team and champion surfers, and this was their first trip to the United States. I asked if they were spending any extra time here after the competition, doing a little sightseeing and the like, but they were moving on early the next morning. They still had a couple more competitions before finishing up the year in Jeffrey's Bay, South Africa. We would head out to J-Bay next month and finish our year-long tour at Bells Beach in Victoria, Australia. We kept the conversation light, mostly focusing on this and other competitions we'd all participated in, how everyone was doing on the waves, and how their Y-T-D scores were shaking out.

After dinner, wait services removed all traces of food and dishes, and the live band moved in. Our group meandered out onto the lanai and the beach, where soft Hawaiian music was piped in. A huge bonfire crackled down by the surf, throwing shadows that danced on the sand like sea spirits. Laughter bubbled up, coming from everywhere on the beach, as spontaneous and capricious as the ocean breeze. A couple of guys wrestled in the sand, their buddies betting on the outcome, while a few others tossed foam footballs back and forth, their whoops and hollers punctuating the night air. I could hear a guitar being strummed and a man singing in accompaniment, people clapping to the beat. We headed that way, and before I knew it, my foot tapped along with the music, my body finding the rhythm.

Like little kids, some people were running around passing out sticks stabbed through the center of marshmallows. Grayson, as excited as a big kid, snagged a few and handed each of us one, his grin as wide as the board he rode.

"I haven't roasted a marshmallow since I was a kid," he said, his voice rough with salt and wind.

We took our treats over toward the bonfire and sat in front of one of the smaller firepits, on many of the blankets scattered about. I held my stick above the embers, rotating the marshmallows, watching them bloat and brown, and then tried to eat the sticky, gooey mess without dropping it or burning my mouth. It was a simple pleasure but as satisfying as a well-ridden wave.

Someone started a game of volleyball a few feet away, and the ball came soaring over the net, landing with a soft thud near my feet. I picked it up, the texture gritty with sand, and we jumped into the game. My movements were spontaneous and exhilarating—a dive, a high-five, the sting of the ball against my palm—all under the gaze of a thousand stars.

There was a shout, "Quinn, to you!" and I launched the ball back over the net, my competitive edge sharpened by the day's defeat and soothed by the night's camaraderie. This was different; there was no prize, no judges, just the pure joy of the game.

After a few rounds, I was hot and thirsty, and I retreated from the game, my breaths deep with the tang of salt air. I got a fresh beer, the liquid cool against my throat, and let out a contented sigh. Laughter, the hiss of surf, the crackle of fire—it was all here, the symphony of a surfer's celebration. The volleyball rolled toward me again, and I tossed it back into the game with a wave, indicating I was out. Boos and hisses greeted my decision, but the game continued without me.

The next morning, most of us slept in, hung over from a night of heavy celebrating. Although I didn't have more than a couple of beers, I didn't crawl out of bed until it was almost time to check out. Luckily, I'd thrown my things together last night before going out with the guys and only needed to shower, get dressed, and check out before time to meet up with the crew downstairs. Sean had called a team meeting for one o'clock in the Dolphin Room, and I had plenty of time to run to the little burger joint around the corner for an old-fashioned, half-pound American cheeseburger with mustard, ketchup, pickles, lettuce, tomatoes, and grilled onions and a sack of crispy fries. I had eaten there every day of the tournament, and after more than a year of being out of the country, I couldn't get enough. They just didn't make burgers—and they just didn't taste the same—anywhere in the world like in the States. Just the thought made my mouth water and my stomach grumble.

CHAPTER
FOUR

After lunch, and everyone had checked out of the hotel, we met in the Dolphin Room before loading onto the bus that would take us back to Los Angeles International Airport.

I dropped my gear next to the mountain of expensive gear and designer luggage the others had piled up against the wall and pulled up a chair at the bare, marble-topped conference table between Jordan and Joey.

"Okay," Sean started, his tone lacking his usual warm camaraderie. Instead, he seemed all business, crisp and firm. "I think we're all here. We won't take up a lot of your time, but Josh and I wanted to take a moment to talk to you before we got out of here."

Josh stood up, his face a mask of professionalism that didn't quite reach his eyes. "I wish we were meeting under different circumstances," he said, his voice steady but somber as he looked over at Sean, who continued with a heavy sigh, "The long and short of it, guys... is that we're disbanding the team. This last year has hit our finances harder than we expected. We are out of reserves, and almost all of our big sponsors have declined to renew our contracts."

A collective gasp sucked the air out of the room. Disbanding? The word ricocheted around inside my skull. This team was my family, my identity.

I felt my grip tighten on the armrests, my knuckles whit-ening. We had ridden waves together, celebrated victories, and supported each other through wipeouts. And now, just like that, we were washing ashore.

Sean made eye contact with each of us before continuing. "We've managed to pull together severance for you all. Josh has taken it upon himself to be very generous, and I think you'll feel it's more than fair." He fanned the stack of envelopes in his hand, then passed them to Josh.

The silence that followed was suffocating. Josh took the en-velopes and came around the table, handing each one of us one, his movements mechanical. When he reached me, our eyes met briefly—a flicker of mutual pain—and he handed me the one on top, my name handwritten across the middle, then moved on.

Sean continued speaking. "We will do all we can to help you get on other teams or make other arrangements. You have our mobile numbers. Feel free to use it."

Holding the envelope in my hand felt like a betrayal. There was a check inside, a generous amount, as Sean had said, but I felt like it was a consolation prize for a game I never agreed to play.

Done with dispensing the envelopes, Josh took his place at the table, standing in front of his chair, and cleared his throat, "We've loved every minute with you guys. This is the hardest decision I've ever had to make."

The room was full of murmurs now, a low tide of disbelief and despair. I couldn't speak, couldn't look up. The walls of the conference room felt like they were closing in, and the future—the one I had envisioned—was being unceremoniously ripped away, leaving behind a void as vast and as unforgiving as the ocean during a storm.

I stared down at the envelope in my hand, the weight of it weighing me down like a stone. The paper crackled, a sound that seemed too loud in the thick silence that had followed the bombshell. Disbanded! The word bounced around in my head, a cruel echo.

My heart pounded a fierce rhythm, the same I felt when dropping into a towering wave, but now it was fear, not adrenaline, that surged through my veins. The air felt heavy, charged with a collective shock that buzzed in my ears and blurred the faces around me.

I squeezed the envelope, the sharp edges pressing into my palm, grounding me in the harsh reality. This thin packet of paper was the full stop at the end of a long, shared sentence. I couldn't open it; to do so would be to acknowledge the finality of it all.

I looked up as Josh and Sean stood there, the weight of their decision carved into the lines of their faces. They were our leaders, the ones who had always navigated us through rough waters, and now they were beaching the ship for good.

I tried to swallow, but my throat was tight, constricted by a swell of emotions. Around me, I heard the rustle of others opening their envelopes, the soft sniffs of those struggling to keep composure. But I was frozen, the envelope clutched in a vice grip, a lifeline that felt more like an anchor dragging me down.

My eyes met Josh's again, and he leaned forward.

"If you ever need anything, Quinn. Call me. We're still family. We'll always be family."

I looked up at him, my eyes meeting his, and I forced myself not to cry. He had to know how much disbanding the team gutted us. I don't know about the others, but I would have stuck with them no matter what. But no words could fix this. No apologies could stitch together the ripped seams of our family. He patted my shoulder and moved on, and I sat motionless, staring at nothing. Silence settled on the room, heavy as the ocean's depths, and in the darkness and silence, I gripped the arms of my chair, my mind racing as frenetic as a storm across the sea. My teammates were shifting, some standing, others clutching their own envelopes like life preservers, but my envelope lay in my lap, unopened. I couldn't go home—not like this, not with hauling a cargo of broken dreams and few options.

My family, my old life, they were a world away—a small coastal community where everyone knew your name and your business. A place I'd left behind with dreams of making it big, of riding waves to glory and bringing back fortunes. The thought of returning, not as the prodigal son made good, but as a castaway, was a bitter pill to swallow. It stuck in my throat.

I couldn't go back to stay with my family, no better than my brother. And I couldn't look into my father's hard, accusing eyes and admit that I had nothing to show for the five years I've been away. It wasn't just pride; it was fear—fear of disappointment, of pity, of being that cautionary tale told to wide-eyed kids with their own dreams of leaving.

The room slowly began to empty, a slow exodus of somber figures, bags and boards slung over shoulders, quiet goodbyes muttered. I barely noticed them leaving. The coach bus that brought us here was waiting in front of the hotel to take us back to L.A.X. if that was where we needed to go. Some people were starting to scramble to arrange flights, purchase tickets home, or a semblance of home. We were no longer on the league's roster, no hotel rooms were reserved for us, and there were no pre-arranged, prepaid flights to take us anywhere. We were on our own. The only silver lining was I was back in the States, in California, but I didn't have a home to go back to. My gaze fixed on the grain of the wooden table, seeing in its pattern the swirls and eddies and currents of the ocean, feeling as adrift as a skiff lost at sea.

I stood up abruptly, my chair scraping against the floor, the back slamming to the floor, the sound loud and painful to my ears. With a deep breath, I stuffed the envelope into my backpack without looking at it. I'd deal with that later when I was alone, and the reality wouldn't sting quite as much. For now, I needed to move, to walk, to breathe. I left the room without looking back.